A MIDNIGHT CLEAR

A LOCUST POINT MYSTERY - BOOK 9

LIBBY HOWARD

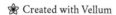 Created with Vellum

CHAPTER 1

I smoothed a hand over the white silk of the full-length, sleeveless dress, lightly tracing the black embroidery across the bodice and down the side as I looked at my reflection. My shoulder-length hair had spent the last hour in hot rollers, making it look like a silver-streaked curly bob. The new do and my professionally applied make-up seemed to take a dozen years off my appearance, but maybe that was wishful thinking on my part. I'd never fretted about my age when Eli had been alive. Growing old was one of the ever-shifting facets of our life and love together. I didn't regret the gray in my hair, or the wrinkles edging my eyes and bracketing my mouth, but it *had* been a shock to look in the mirror after Eli's funeral and wonder where the last few decades had gone. One moment I was forty, and the next I was sixty, a widow, and worried that I'd need to sell our beloved home before I even had a chance to order the head-stone for my husband's grave.

I wished Eli could see me now. Actually, I wished the Eli prior to his accident could see me now. The Eli I'd been married to the last ten years of our lives would have felt a pang of regret to see this woman in the mirror. There had been moments when he'd expressed equal parts guilt and frustration over his condition, and claimed that he was nothing more than a heavy stone around my neck, weighing me down. He'd worried that his disability was eating away at our marriage.

That hadn't been true. Yes, there were days when caring for him was hard. There were times when he seemed so different from who he'd been before the accident. But together we'd found a different kind of love than we'd had in the first part of our marriage.

Even though I tried to let my memories be a balm to the grief, there were days when the realization that he was gone stabbed sharply in my chest. I'd let him go. I hadn't seen or felt his ghost since Thanksgiving. And although I knew that was the right thing, I missed the comfort his ghostly presence brought me.

Tonight felt like a turning point somehow. It felt as if I were taking a step forward out of the old and into something new and different—into something scary.

The woman staring back at me from out of the mirror appeared strong, confident, smart, beautiful—not beautiful like a girl in the first blush of womanhood, or a mother glowing with the frazzled beauty of one who creates and nurtures. No, this woman in the mirror had maturity. She had the beauty of a woman who has seen life, who knows what she wants, who sees through bullshit and isn't about to let anyone—man or woman—take advantage of her.

She was sexy. And that's what scared me.

I didn't need to be sexy. Okay, a tiny part of me wanted to be sexy, but I didn't *need* it. Not now. Maybe not ever.

There was a little devil on my shoulder that called me a liar. I'd never been a beauty, but at sixty I felt as if I were closer to that adjective than I'd ever been. I knew that I would turn heads tonight. I knew that even in a culture that worshiped the cult of youth when it came to women, I would be seen, respected, admired, and desired. The little devil on my shoulder was excited about that.

Actually the little devil was excited to see one man's reaction in particular.

What would Judge Beck say when he saw me? Unbidden, my imagination flew off into scenes of intimacy I had no business thinking of.

Yes, he was a very handsome man. These months living with him had revealed him to be kind, honorable, intelligent, fair, and caring. He had a sense of humor. He was an amazing father. If I were to be completely honest with myself, I'd been fighting an attraction to him for quite a while now. But I worried that falling in love with the judge would only end in heartbreak for me. He was nearly fifteen years younger than me. He wasn't divorced yet, and I wasn't quite sure he was ready to move on from his failed marriage at this time. Even if some miracle occurred and he felt a spark of attraction for me, anything between us would be doomed to failure. I'd end up not just with heartbreak. I'd lose two kids I'd grown to love. I'd lose a friendship and companionship I'd come to cherish. I'd lose a roommate and the income that kept my house from foreclosure.

I'd buried my husband less than a year ago. How could I possibly be thinking of another man so soon? What sort of horrible, disloyal wife was I to even *think* about a relationship with another man at this time?

Glancing at the clock, I realized it was time to go. I straightened my shoulders, smoothed a hand once more down my dress, and turned away from the mirror. The stairs creaked as I headed down. Turning on the final landing, I caught a glimpse of Taco, Henry, and Madison, waiting at the bottom of the stairs. Henry grinned, giving me a less-than-subtle thumbs-up. Madison's eyes grew wide, her mouth in an "O". Then she did what I can only describe as a quick jig. Taco wasn't as impressed. The cat eyed me, then proceeded to sit down and clean one of his paws.

"She's ready!" Madison announced, still hopping from one foot to the other.

Two more steps down and Judge Beck came into my view. His back was toward me, a tall, muscular figure in black, his blond hair not quite short enough to hide the natural wave that curled the lighter bits around the back of his neck. He turned at his daughter's words, and my breath lodged in my chest.

I'd seen him in suits. I'd seen him in his judge's robes. I'd seen him in khakis and a polo shirt, in swimming trunks, in pajama bottoms with an old t-shirt, but nothing compared to Judge Beck in a tux. Holy cow, the man should have been a model for formal wear.

I'm sure it helped that the tux was obviously not a rental, and had been clearly designed and tailored not just to fit his body, but to accentuate his broad shoulders and slim waist. The back view had been darned fine, but from the front…

I forced my eyes up to his face, and felt my legs turn to rubber. That one lock of blond hair had escaped the rest and staked a claim on his forehead, giving him a look of disheveled glamor. The tanned skin with his chiseled good looks. The curve of his mouth that softened all but the sternest of his expressions. Everything about him breathtakingly handsome, but it was his eyes that truly held me—those beautiful hazel eyes.

Suddenly I realized I was standing on the steps like a statue, staring at my roommate while two teens eyed us both in amusement.

Do not *fall down the stairs*. I forced myself to take a

cautious step, holding the railing just in case my unexpectedly weak legs failed me.

"You look very nice, Kay," Judge Beck told me in a husky tone.

Madison rolled her eyes and shot her father an exasperated glance. "You look beautiful in that dress, Kay. Doesn't she, Dad?"

"Yes. The dress is very nice."

I bit back a smile, feeling more confident now that I knew my appearance had turned the usually well-spoken Judge Beck into a man who only knew one, rather lame, adjective.

"Thank you. I found it in the back of my closet and can't remember when I must have bought it." I shook my head, thinking I deserved an Emmy nomination for this. "It's probably been in there for a decade at least."

Madison did *not* deserve an Emmy nomination. She laughed, clapping a hand over her mouth as she did that little jig again. I ignored her and walked over to the judge, picking my clutch up off the table and trying to smile up at him as if he wasn't an Adonis of a man, as if we were just two friends heading out for a work function, or some charity event.

He took a step forward, and suddenly we were too close. I wasn't sure what to do, so I tucked my clutch under my arm and reached up and straightened his tie that most definitely didn't need straightening.

"You look quite handsome in that tux, Judge Beck," I told him, refusing to use the word *nice*.

"You, too. In the dress, I mean. Not tux. Very nice." He drew in a ragged breath and ran a hand over his hair, freeing a few additional renegade locks to curl across his forehead. "We'll probably be late," he said to Madison and Henry. "We might not get back until well after midnight."

"Yes, yes." Madison's entire posture screamed that typical

teen *whatever*. "We both have our phones. We're to stay in the house and call if there's any problem."

"No, you're to call your mother if there's any problem," Judge Beck reminded her.

"Or Miss Daisy," Henry added. "Since she's right down the street and can be here super fast in case we catch the house on fire or accidently fall on top of a butcher knife, or some dude in a hockey mask with a chainsaw tries to kill us."

"Stop." I laughed. "You're going to freak your father out, and we'll never get to this Christmas party. No fires, or playing with butcher knives. And no opening the door to horror movie villains. Okay?"

Henry held up a hand. "I promise."

"We better get going, before I decide I need to hire a babysitter." Judge Beck pulled my wrap from the back of a chair, draping it over my shoulders and letting his fingers linger just a second on my neck as I hooked the clasp to secure it.

"Taco has already been out," I reminded the kids, struggling not to lose myself to the feel of what was probably an accidental caress as the judge removed his hands. "Not too many treats, and don't let him convince you he hasn't been fed, because he has."

The kids promised to not be conned by my cat as Judge Beck put a hand on my lower back to guide me to the door. I felt the heat and pressure through the silk of my dress and shivered. He kept the contact until we were outside, hesitating until he heard the kids lock up behind us before walking beside me down the wide stairs of my old Victorian home. We'd had a cold snap, and the frost on the sidewalk crunched under my pumps as we made our way to the judge's SUV. His hand came out to take my elbow, and I appreciated the gesture. It had been a while since I'd worn more than modest heels, and I was a little uncertain how slippery the sidewalk would be.

He opened the door, waiting for me to step into the SUV and get myself settled before closing the door and heading around to the driver's side. The judge had always been polite and charmingly old fashioned in his manners, but this felt odd, as if we were two awkward kids on our way to the senior prom.

We were silent as the slick black SUV pulled out of the driveway and headed down the street. I was determined to break the silence, and scrambled for something to talk about that would serve as a sort of ice-breaker between us.

"What are you getting the kids for Christmas?" I finally asked.

He chuckled, his long fingers sliding along the steering wheel as he turned the corner. "Madison wants a car."

"So you'll be buying her a purse? Or a leather-bound set of law books?"

"She's mature, a good student, and she's been a careful driver."

"But?" I eyed him, biting back a smile.

"I keep thinking about that party she snuck out to this past spring. I hate to not trust her, but it would be a whole lot easier for her to do that with her own car."

"I think they have some sort of parental control GPS things you can put in cars now," I told him. "Her phone as well."

"I know. There *would* be benefits to her having her own car as far as logistics in sports and school activities but I can't help but feel absolutely terrified at the thought that she might be in an accident, hurt, or possibly killed. She's not an experienced driver, and all it would take is one moment of indecision or inattention and that person running a stop sign or drifting across the center line will hit her."

"You'll eventually have to trust her to drive your and Heather's cars solo, even if you don't buy her one of her own," I pointed out.

"Yes, but I don't have to like it." He sighed and shook his head. "This is just as frightening as when we brought her home from the hospital, a tiny little baby that I worried was going to stop breathing at any moment. It's just as frightening as that time Henry fell and hit his head on the corner of the coffee table. It's just as frightening as that time I found some man trying to kill you in the house across the street."

I took a moment to process that, perversely glad that I'd made the cut of people whose possible deaths frightened him.

"And I hate the expectation that kids should be getting a brand new car the moment they get their licenses. I didn't have a car until I was eighteen, and even then it was an Oldsmobile sedan made the year I was born that had mismatched seats and a broken fuel gauge."

"So you didn't have to fake the whole 'Oh my, I've run out of gas' thing on a date?" I teased.

He laughed. "I was too afraid of being chased down the street by some angry father waving a shotgun to try that one. Basically I topped the gas tank off every three days, terrified that I'd end up stranded on some back road and wind up a victim of the guy with the hockey mask and the chainsaw."

I nodded. "Wise choice. My first car was a 1972 Ford Pinto wagon complete with wood paneled sides. It was the mini-version of the big old family station wagons of the seventies. Like your car, my fuel gauge was faulty, although mine worked fine until it got to a quarter of a tank, then it stuck. First time I ran out of gas, I was convinced something else was wrong with the car because it still said I had a quarter tank of gas. Of course it had said I had a quarter tank of gas for almost two weeks. It never crossed my mind that my Pinto wagon wasn't going to be getting sixty miles a gallon."

"Maybe I should get Madison a '72 Pinto wagon, although one with a working gas gauge," he suggested.

"The gas gauge would be the least of your problems. I doubt you could find one still running. They weren't exactly built to last, you know."

We drove for a few miles in silence before Judge Beck spoke again. "Heather asked me to get her the car. She said she'd chip in what she could afford and it would be from 'both of us'."

I didn't know how to respond to that. I liked the judge's soon-to-be ex-wife, but I knew their divorce was stuffed full of anger, regret, and feelings of betrayal. I also knew that unless he was digging his heels in on something strictly out of anger and pride, that I'd always support his point of view —although I always tried to gently suggest a compromise.

"What did you reply?" I ended up asking.

"That I'd think about it." He shot me a wry look. "And yes, my knee-jerk reaction was that I shouldn't have to include Heather if I'm paying for ninety percent of the gift."

I shifted in the seat to face him. "What's the real stumbling block? Is it that Heather wants this for Madison and you're feeling contrary? Is it that you truly don't think she's ready for her own car and maybe she needs a few years of driving experience under her belt first? Fears for her safety? A philosophical stance that children shouldn't have their own cars until they're eighteen? Worry over the expense?"

"All of the above." He shrugged. "I think I'd be willing to get her a used beater car to learn on. Something sturdy that won't break the bank if she rubs a tire on the curb or backs into a concrete support in a parking garage. That way she could call it her own and she'd have some flexibility about meeting friends and going to sporting events without needing to take our only vehicle."

"So do it." I reached out and tugged playfully at the sleeve of his tux. "I'll start searching Craigslist for '72 Pinto wagons. Heather will only need to contribute a couple of twenties at the most, and you can slap a bow on it for Christmas and make a young woman happy."

"I know you're joking, but the whole 'used car' thing is also a problem." He frowned. "I floated the idea to Heather and she was appalled. Evidently the kids at the high school either get a brand new car or none at all. I don't really care if Heather thinks it's beneath us to give our child a used car, but I don't want Madison to hate it, to be disappointed."

I reached out again to touch his sleeve. "Do you *know* your daughter? Yes, Madison loves her fancy clothes and shoes and make-up. Yes, she wants to run with the popular crowd and date the hot boys, but when it comes down to it, she's well-grounded. She sticks up for her friends, hangs out with kids who share her interests no matter if they're rich or popular or not. She befriended Peony Smith, for goodness sake. And she's continued to write to her and encourage her even after the girl went to prison. She's not going to turn her nose up at a used car. I mean, maybe she would if you got her a '72 Pinto wagon, but not a twelve-year-old Acura or something."

The judge chuckled. "You know Henry would be all about that '72 Pinto wagon."

I laughed in response. "Henry would restore that sucker and be the envy of the whole school. That boy marches to the beat of his own drum and I love him for that."

Judge Beck glanced my way, an unreadable expression on his face. "Really?"

I felt a warm glow—the same warm glow I felt every time I thought of my roommate and his children. "I love both

Madison and Henry. I'd do anything for those kids, you know that. I hope that when you eventually get your own place and move away they'll come by and visit me, invite me to their special events, maybe even friend me on Facebook or Snapchat or something. I can't imagine going through the rest of my life without them in it."

"I'm...I'm glad you feel that way about them." His voice was soft, full of some sort of meaning I couldn't discern.

"Get Madison a reasonably priced used car. Something safe, but cool in a chic, retro kind of way. She'll love it, in spite of what Heather says." Part of the reason she'd love it was because it came from her father. Madison adored her dad. It was understandable. There was a lot about the man to adore.

"What about Henry?" I added. "What does he want for Christmas?"

A warm smile creased the judge's face. "A snowboard with boots, bindings, and appropriate clothing. Oh, and a season's pass at Wildwood Mountain."

Henry loved antiques, online gaming, and cats, but he did participate in the occasional sport. He wasn't quite as skilled as his sister, but he'd been on the track and field team this past spring. Snowboarding? I could see him enjoying that.

"I've got a surprise for the kids this Christmas. I'm thinking about a family trip out to Aspen in January. Henry can still snowboard here locally, but it's time for us to have a family vacation—our *new* family now that Heather's and my divorce is nearly final."

"How are you going to manage the time off work?" I waved my hand at his outfit. "Plus we're going to this party because you're being considered for an appellate judgeship at the state level. Won't taking a week off next month interfere with your...campaign or whatever it is you need to do?"

"As for my current responsibilities, I can make sure my

schedule accommodates a week off. It's not like I can't take briefs and summaries with me to review in the evenings."

I frowned at that. "Seriously? On vacation with your kids?"

"I know, I know, but if I have to do it, I will. I'd prefer to do nothing but ski, enjoy some time with my children, drink wine in the hot tub, and sit by the fire."

It sounded ideal, and I longed to go with them. I hadn't hit the slopes in decades, but I'd be willing to blow the dust off the old skis in the basement and give it a try. I envisioned laughing with Madison and Henry on the lifts, big clouds of powder rising from the ground as I flew down the hills, drinking wine in the hot tub with the judge, sitting by the fire with the judge.

And other things that I didn't want to acknowledge I was thinking about.

"I think they'll both love that." I tried to keep the yearning from my voice. They *would* love it. Both kids clearly cherished every moment they spent with their dad.

"And the appellate judgeship..." Judge Beck shrugged. "I'm not sure that I'm even a serious contender for that position. There are other older, more qualified candidates who have been able to rub elbows with the right people for decades. Tonight is a long shot. After tonight I'll know if I've got a chance at getting this position or not."

"And if you do?" I asked, eyeing him.

His hands tightened on the steering wheel. "If I do, well then I'll need to think about whether taking a week to go to Jackson Hole would be feasible or not."

CHAPTER 2

$\mathcal{W}$ e pulled up to an eight-story building that looked more like a posh hotel than an office. A man in a bellhop-style uniform jumped forward to open my door, another opening the judge's and handing him a paper slip for his valet parking. Judge Beck met me around the front of the SUV and once again put a hand on my back as we climbed the marble stairs that lead to a landing then up to a huge set of glass double doors.

Two armed security guards stood on the landing, their eyes sweeping over the us as we approached. The judge gave them our names and one of them consulted his cell phone while the other murmured something into a small walkie-talkie device.

The guard with the cell phone nodded, while a voice on the other end of the walkie-talkie confirmed we were indeed on the invitation list. I'd been to some fancy parties before, but never one with quite this level of security.

"Is the president here or something?" I whispered as we moved past the guards and continued to climb the stairs.

"I doubt it. The governor might be here, as well as state

senators and representatives, mayors, delegates. It's a big deal to be invited."

"What sort of law do these people practice?" I asked, hearing the noise of conversation and violins as another pair of armed guards opened the heavy glass doors for us.

"All kinds. They have a division for criminal law, one for patent applications, one for contract law. You name it. Most of their fame has come from a few well-known class action suits."

"Like the long-distance carrier lawsuit?" I'd read articles on the Cresswell settlement a few decades back, and remembered that Sullivan, Morris, Stein and Callahan was the firm involved in that case.

"Yes, that was one of their most well-known lawsuits. Class action is a long game with potential big wins, but more often moderate losses. It's other divisions that make SMS&C the majority of their money."

"Isn't one of their attorneys up for the appellate position?"

I'd done some research knowing that Judge Beck had invited me to this party because I was smart and savvy, and that I could network and potentially help him in career advancement. It would be easier for me to do that if I knew who the movers and shakers were, as well as Judge Beck's competition for the appellate seat.

"He's the forerunner for the opening," Judge Beck murmured, cutting off the conversation and nodding to the two gentlemen wearing the same uniforms as the valets.

They checked our identification, and once more consulted an electronic guest list as the buzz of conversation, the sound of violins, the clink of glasses, and the occasional laughter swirled around us. Judge Beck took my arm as we walked toward a coat check.

I unclasped my wrap and Judge Beck handed it to the coat check woman, passing the ticket over to me. It all seemed so old fashioned. I hadn't attended an event like this since before Eli's accident, and even then I'd managed my own coat check. I eyed the judge, wondering if he would be fetching drinks for me, communicating my order to wait-staff, pulling out chairs for me and standing every time I returned from the restroom like a hero in a nineteen forties movie. I wasn't sure how I felt about all this. In some ways it was charming, but I still felt uncomfortable, as if I were suddenly transported back sixty years and considered the weaker sex.

Thankfully I didn't have much time to think about it because seconds later we were in an atrium-type foyer that had been converted into the party room. It was a huge space, connected to the second floor by a wide marble staircase. Looking up I could see a walkway lining the edges of the atrium with glass-walled office spaces that I assumed would be filled with expensive furniture and expensive limited-edition artwork.

"How many floors does SMS&C have of this building?" I asked the judge as we both looked around the room.

"Second and third," he replied. "They rent the atrium for this party, but the offices down those halls belong to some tax accounting firm. At least they did the last time I was here."

I looked around, wondering how the tenants on the upper floors got to their offices. Stairways besides this marble-and-gilt one in the atrium were probably at the far ends of the building behind gray steel doors, but there had to be an elevator somewhere.

I couldn't see any elevator, but the ostentatious staircase was roped off with velvet cord, confining the party to the atrium. The room was plenty large enough, even though it looked as if nearly a hundred people were milling about, chatting in groups and drinking an assortment of what I was sure were alcoholic beverages. I saw a small bar set-up off to the side, and a host of people in catering uniforms setting up chafing dishes full of food. In the rear near the staircase was a small stage with a string quartet who were currently playing "God Rest Ye Merry Gentlemen".

The security seemed confined to the outside of the building, but I was sure a few of the tuxedoed and suited gentlemen here might be unobtrusively carrying weapons as they watched the crowd for threats to any of the political bigwigs in attendance.

"Is the governor here?" I asked, pretty sure I wouldn't be able to recognize the man if I saw him.

"I don't see him." Judge Beck did another quick scan of the room. "Katherine Nguyen is over by the staircase talking to Mayor Buchenheimer though.

I glanced over at the lieutenant governor and the mayor of the capital, noting a stern-faced, muscled man standing nearby.

"Shall we?" Judge Beck extended an elbow toward me. I entwined my arm in his, feeling a twinge of nervousness as we descended into the crowd.

"I don't know some of these people, so if I don't introduce you, assume that I either don't know them or can't remember their name," Judge Beck murmured into my ear. "The key people I'll want to talk to tonight are those from SMS&C since they're our hosts, the state appeals court judges, those who are also candidates for the opening, and some of the local judges."

I glanced around as the sea of unfamiliar faces and spotted one I knew. "There's Judge Sanchez."

Judge Beck's eyebrows shot up and he grinned. "You know him?"

"I know *of* him. I killed some time as a spectator in his courtroom a few months back, and of course I see his name on paperwork here and there. I'm sure he's got no idea who I am."

"Well, he's about to." The judge steered me deftly through the crowd. It put us practically against each other. His jacket brushed my side as we walked, his shoulder nudging mine with each step. It felt intimate and completely natural.

We never made it to Judge Sanchez—at least not then. Twenty steps forward and someone called Judge Beck's name. He halted, greeting the approaching group, and I realized that Judge Sanchez wasn't the only person here I recognized. I didn't know these people's names, but I'd seen them before. Specifically I'd seen them on the golf course at the fill-the-food-bank charity golf tournament that Matt had put on this fall.

Judge Beck shook hands and slapped shoulders, then turned and introduced them to me.

Clifford Dorvinski, Damien Smith, and Horace Barnes, all partners at the local law firm Smith, Barnes and Dorvinski. Better known on the golf course as the Legal Eagles Team.

I smiled and found myself making small talk with Horace Barnes while the judge spoke with the other two. Horace was bald, his face full of wrinkles and brown spots that told me he'd enjoyed a whole lot of his life outside without sunscreen. His shoulders had narrowed and drooped with age, but something about their set made me think he'd once been a strong and fit man. There was a gold signet ring on the hand he extended to shake mine, and I wondered if it was a family antique or from his college days.

"Enjoying the party, Mrs. Carerra?" The man's light blue eyes blinked at me from behind thick, black-rimmed glasses that looked as if he'd been wearing them since 1960.

"We just got here." I glanced over at the string quartet. "It's a beautiful venue, though. Lovely music."

He sniffed. "Music. Food. Booze. That's about it. It's a party where the main purpose is to see and be seen, to brown-nose your way up the legal, political, or judicial ladder. That's why Nate's here, no doubt."

I shrugged, thinking the man was terribly doom-and-gloom given the holiday season. "I don't see any reason why we can't enjoy ourselves at functions that mix work and social time. Besides, networking is a vital part of every career. When I was a journalist, *who* I knew was sometimes more important than *what* I knew. It got me information that others didn't get, and sometimes gave me the scoop on breaking stories. Yes, sometimes business functions can seem unsavory, but making connections does provide additional opportunities."

He frowned. "You're a journalist? I thought Nate told me that you were an internet detective or something."

Judge Beck hadn't mentioned what my career was when he'd introduced me just now. It startled me a bit to realize that not only had the judge mentioned me before to these local lawyers, but that Horace Barnes had remembered. Although I got the impression not much escaped Horace Barnes' notice.

"I used to be a journalist. I had to go freelance about ten years ago, then this past year I joined an investigative agency doing skip tracing. I just received my PI license."

He nodded sagely. "Journalism doesn't pay much anymore unless you can turn it into a political exposé novel. Huh. Maybe you can write true crime novels like that famous woman. What agency do you work for?"

"Pierson Investigative and Recovery Services."

"Good Lord! Don't tell me you work for that ridiculous man with the internet video channel. What's he call himself? Crocodile or something?"

I bit back a retort. My boss's YouTube nickname was

Gator—Gator Pierson. But I wasn't about to bother correcting Horace Barnes on that, when there was something far more important I needed to set him straight about.

"Gone are the days when a business could market by just a listing in the Yellow Pages and possibly an ad in the local newspaper. Potential clients are on the internet. If a business wants visibility and growth, then they need have an online presence in a variety of social media sites which include YouTube."

"I think that's what my grandkids would call a 'burn', Horace," Clifford Dorvinski joked. I looked around and noticed that the other two lawyers as well as Judge Beck had overheard my statement.

Drat. He'd brought me here because he'd thought I'd be socially savvy around a bunch of cutthroat lawyers, and the first one I met I ended up in a disagreement with. We weren't throwing punches or anything, but still I really didn't need to hurt Judge Beck's chances by being combative. Glancing over at the judge, I expected to see a horrified expression, not a barely suppressed grin.

"Get your law degree and we'll hire you," Damien Smith said with a nod.

"Heck no. Hire her now as our marketing manager," Clifford replied. "Maybe we'd get a few new clients that weren't on the other side of sixty."

I was sixty and hated the stereotype that anyone my age couldn't figure out technology newer than a flip phone, but I decided I'd done quite enough arguing for tonight.

"I'm not doing YouTube videos," Horace complained. "Or that Instagram stuff either. The only reason I'm on Facebook is because it's the only way I can see pictures of my grandsons playing baseball. Otherwise all I'd get is a few school photos with the annual Christmas card."

"I think we need to dress Horace up in a shark costume

and run video ads," Damien announced. "Give that Gator Pierson a run for his money. He might have murder, repossessions, and bail jumpers, but we've got land title disputes, insurance fraud, and inheritance lawsuits. Far more interesting stuff, in my opinion."

Everyone laughed—me as well even though I personally thought there probably *was* interesting stuff in land title disputes, insurance fraud, and inheritance lawsuits. I guess it was the journalist in me as well as the newly licensed detective, but I saw all sorts of intriguing possibilities for investigation in those crimes.

Conversation turned to something about recent court decisions regarding intellectual property. After a few minutes, Judge Beck leaned down and mentioned something about food and a drink. We excused ourselves, but encountered Judge Sanchez and a woman he introduced as his wife Justine before we could make it to the buffet line. I immediately hit it off with the pair, loving the judge's dry humor and finding a common interest in gardening with his wife. Justine and I ended up showing each other pictures of our cats, exchanging numbers, and promising to meet for lunch on Tuesday before Judge Beck once more attempted to get us to where the food and drink were being doled out.

I had absolutely no idea what the little tiny hors d'oeuvres contained, but put half a dozen of them on my plate and moved on to take a glass of wine from the bartender. It wasn't going to be easy juggling a drink in one hand and trying to eat from a plate with the other, but our hosts had sacrificed space for all but about five dining tables for standing room, so there was no other choice. I was regretting my white dress and hoping none of the little canapés I'd grabbed had mustard or anything that might stain the silk when we encountered another group whom the judge seemed to know.

After a few greetings and handshakes, the judge turned to me. "Let me introduce my friend Kay Carrera, who is a private investigator specializing in skip traces and internet research."

Seven pairs of eyes turned to me, all of them filled with respect. It was then I realized that the judge had referred to me as a friend, and that he'd made me sound like I was the female version of a modern-day Dick Tracy. Suddenly, I realized that this evening wasn't just a networking opportunity for him, it was one for me as well.

Each of these lawyers, judges, and politicians was a potential client. J.T. had quite a few local lawyers who contracted investigative work to him on behalf of their clients. If any of the people I met tonight ended up calling us, not only would we have more business, but I'd also get a finder's fee. Immediately my thoughts strayed to the furnace, the roof, my old sedan that I started every morning with hope and a prayer.

Judge Beck made introductions, and I struggled to remember the ten names being thrown at me at once. Several were partners at Sullivan, Morris, Stein and Callahan, and thus our hosts for the evening. To those lawyers I expressed my admiration for the venue, the food, drink, and music, knowing that partners in such a huge multi-divisional law firm were unlikely to need to call on a small-town private investigator. The others were Judge Rhett Reynolds and Ruby Reynolds, Irene O'Donnell, and Judge Sonny Magoo.

Sonny Magoo had full head of gorgeous silver hair, and a tan that looked natural enough to hint at a recent trip to the islands. I knew that he was a state appellate court judge, and immediately realized his opinion would be a factor in whether Judge Beck got the opening or not.

Judge Reynolds was a large florid man in his fifties with a perpetual smile. Instead of the plain black bow tie most attendees sported, his was embellished with brightly colored, gilt-edged candy canes. Ruby Reynolds was also large with an equally cheerful smile. She was quite a bit younger than Judge Reynolds, but I couldn't tell if she was his wife, his daughter, or if she just shared a last name with the man. Unfortunately Judge Beck's introductions didn't specify, and there wasn't time for clarification before one of the partners at SMS&C began ribbing Judge Reynolds on his attendance.

"Didn't think you'd be gracing us with your presence, Rhett," another partner teased. "You refuse to come every year. Isn't your attendance a violation of your strict ethics code?"

"Maybe he's going to stand up on stage and subject us to an hour-long lecture on conflict of interest," another joked.

"I'm shocked security let him in after what he said about police corruption last week." The tall woman who'd been introduced to me as Irene O'Donnell, a lawyer at SMS&C took a healthy gulp of her wine after the statement.

Judge Rhett Reynolds put an arm around Ruby and squeezed her shoulder. "I thought it would be a good opportunity for Ruby to get out of the office and rub elbows with people outside of our county. Besides, the shrimp cocktail here is legendary."

The woman beamed up at the older man before shifting her smile to Irene and the others. "I'll admit I did pester him to come tonight. It's not like I get many chances to wear a formal gown, you know."

"It *is* a beautiful gown." I admired the emerald green satin dress that hugged the woman's bosom, then flared out into a wide sweep at her waist. "You look lovely."

She did. The jewel tone of the gown was the perfect accent to her golden skin, black hair and dark eyes.

A dimple creased her cheek. "Thank you. I love your dress. That embroidery is so striking and elegant."

Judge Beck touched my elbow and I turned to join him in conversation with Sonny Magoo and Rebecca Stein, one of the partners of SMS&C.

"So you're a private investigator," Judge Magoo asked me. "That must be exciting."

I laughed. "Not as much as the television shows make it out to be. I spend most of my day doing background checks and skip traces. So much investigative work is done over the internet that I have little time for running down criminals in back alleyways."

"Or taking pictures of a straying husband and his mistress through a hotel window?" He glanced over at a woman in a bright red dress a few feet away as he said that, making me wonder if she was the one cheating or the mistress.

"Thankfully I haven't had to do that."

"So are you here tonight on business or pleasure?"

I got an uncomfortable feeling from this man. He seemed bland and jovial enough, but there was something in his eyes that made me think he was digging for information. Was he trying to find something out about Judge Beck that might sway his opinion on my roommate as a candidate for the opening? I couldn't think of any other reason he would be carefully maneuvering around whatever the heck it was he wanted to know.

"A little of both." Did he need a private investigator? It seemed gauche to offer him my card in the middle of a party.

"Be careful who you talk to, Ms. Carrera. There are people here who have an agenda and are full of lies. Make sure you take everything you might hear with a healthy dose of skepticism."

And with that he turned and began to talk to one of the law firm partners. I filed the weird comments away and tried to join in the general conversation. Suddenly the evening became work and I found myself having to listen attentively and make non-committal comments concerning legal policy I knew nothing about. I held my own, but breathed a sigh of relief when Irene O'Donnell tugged me aside.

"So you and Judge Beck..." Her words trailed off with a lift of a thin, sculpted brow and a toss of her long, auburn hair.

"We're friends." I sipped my wine frantically thinking of how I could change the topic before she started grilling me on my or the judge's personal life.

"Friends? Really?" The other sculpted eyebrow rose to join the first.

"Really. He wanted to attend and knew I'd be thrilled for the opportunity to expand my potential client base." I thought the salesy approach would scare her off, but I under-estimated Irene O'Donnell.

"I'll admit I wanted to throw my bra in the ring when I heard about his divorce, but I figured he'd go the fake-boobs, twenty-something, blonde route though. I gotta admit my respect for the guy went up considerably when I saw him walk in with you. He's smoking hot and on a fast-track for success. He could have any woman he wanted. To pick an older woman, even one who's attractive and sharp as a tack, takes the kind of long-term planning that most men lack. Ninety-nine percent of them think with their dicks. And if it wasn't for the old boys' network, they'd all be begging on a street corner right now, or behind bars before they were forty."

"So what kind of cases do you handle for SMS&C?" I asked, desperate to change the conversation.

Irene laughed, revealing ultra-white teeth between her dark-red lips. "Okay. I get it. I was hoping for some juicy gossip, or perhaps something to rekindle the hope in my cold shriveled heart that I might be able to get that judge in the sack. Or at least get a dinner out of him. Guess not." She polished off the contents of her glass before answering my question. "DWI. I'm a minnow in the shark tank of SMS&C. Admittedly, I make some serious cash for the firm, but getting Daddy Warbucks' precious little girl off with a PBJ doesn't exactly earn me respect from the old white guys who run this place."

I was beginning to think this hadn't been Irene's first glass of wine.

"Well, if you come across a case where you feel your client could benefit from some investigative resources—perhaps you suspect a spiked drink, or other situation—please keep me in mind." I eyed Judge Beck out of the corner of my eye, wondering how I could extricate myself from this conversation without drawing him away from the appellate court judge he was speaking with.

Irene eyed her empty glass, as if she couldn't imagine ever needing my services. Then she froze, lifting her dark eyes to glance at the others before meeting mine.

"You know...there is something you might be able to help me with. Looks like you could use another glass of wine. Join me at the bar?"

Intrigued, I nodded and followed her, giving Judge Beck a quick pat on the arm and an inclined head to show him where I was heading. I didn't have a lot of hope for any future business with Irene, but she didn't appear so drunk that she was in danger of falling down or throwing up, and I got the feeling she was a font of gossip.

I did love gossip. As we headed to the bar I wondered what completely unorthodox and blunt thing she'd say next.

"Judge Reynolds is a dick," she announced as she flagged down the bartender and motioned for two more glasses of wine. "He rules over that podunk county courthouse in the west of the state like he's a king. But that's where the university is, which means that's where the majority of my clients are."

So, no juicy gossip after all, just a lawyer and a judge who didn't get along. As much as I wanted to bring in new clients, I wasn't going to take a case that required me to dig up dirt on a county judge for revenge purposes.

"I don't think I can help you with that." I turned as if I were about to move away.

Irene put out a hand motioning me to stay. "Hear me out. He's always bringing the hammer down on my cases. I want him out of that county. He's nominated for that appellate court opening, but he'll never get it—not when Judge Dixon is one of the votes."

I wasn't sure where she was going with any of this, but was curious enough to ask a few questions. "Why wouldn't Judge Dixon vote for him? And how do you propose to unseat him? No judge has lost a public confidence vote in decades. The only other way for him to lose his position is if he were disbarred."

Or dead, but I was pretty sure Irene wasn't going there, drunk or not.

"Well, he banged Judge Dixon's wife. She's that blonde over there in the red talking to Trent Elliott. Reynolds screwed her, then dumped her. No one likes to be made a cuckold. Amusing as the whole situation was, it means as long as Judge Dixon is alive, Reynolds isn't going to be getting serious consideration for an appellate seat."

"How did Judge Reynolds' wife feel about that whole thing?" I snuck a peek over at the man in question as well as the woman who'd been introduced to me as Ruby Reynolds.

"The guy's been divorced for over a decade. I doubt if his wife cares one flying fig what he does with his pecker."

Irene paused in her story to accept the glasses of wine

from the bartender. I'd expected her to pass one over to me, but she kept them both for herself, sipping from the one in her left hand. I glanced again at Ruby Reynolds. Sister? Cousin? Daughter? If Ruby was his ex-wife, then her relationship with her ex-husband couldn't be all that acrimonious since she was attending as his guest and he had his arm around her shoulder.

"Anyway." Irene waved a wine glass, miraculously not spilling a drop. "I want to hire you to find out all you can on the guy. Anything that might get him bounced from his seat, you know? Something like kiddy porn or a weird fetish, or exchanging a favorable ruling for sex. Salacious stuff works best. Or drugs. No one cares about white collar crime anymore."

"That's not really the sort of investigative work that we do," I told her, even though we'd done that exact sort of investigation all the time in divorce cases. I wasn't thrilled about those jobs either, but this was definitely a job I'd turn down before it even got to J.T.'s ears.

"How about—"

"It was so nice meeting you! Bye." I left her at the bar with her two wine glasses and headed back to where Judge Beck was still speaking with Judge Magoo. Not wanting to interrupt them, I lingered and found myself next to Ruby Reynolds.

"Quite the shindig, huh?" she said with a smile and a shake of her head. "I can't help but calculate the cost of all this in my head. I'm sure SMS&C can afford it, but as a rural, small-town attorney, it's a bit overwhelming."

"It's your first time at this party, too?" I turned to face her. "I heard Judge Reynolds doesn't usually attend, but have you been invited before?"

"Oh, heck no." She chuckled. "Dad gets invited every year. They tend to shell out invites to all the judges whether they attend or not. I'm here as his plus-one. There's no way these bigwigs even know who I am."

Ah. His daughter. That made sense even though I couldn't see any resemblance between them aside from their shape and similar smiles.

"I'm a plus-one as well," I confessed. "And I'm pretty sure ninety percent of the people here have no idea who I am either."

"Keeping the female sharks away from Judge Beck?" she guessed. "Making sure his reputation remains unsullied in the wake of his divorce?"

"I'm pretty sure he's able to keep the sharks away all on his own," I drawled, glancing over at the judge. He was still talking with Sonny Magoo, completely oblivious to the various women who were shooting admiring glances his way.

"I'm sure he is." She smiled. "He's got a good reputation, you know. The man is well known for being collaborative when it comes to working with other judges, lawyers, politicians, and the public. He really listens and applies the spirit of the law, not just the letter. He has a reputation for putting forth his opinions, but in a way that doesn't get his adversaries grabbing for the pitchforks. Plus he's got a fifties sitcom personal life outside of the divorce—which shocked the heck out of everyone by the way."

I glanced once more toward Judge Beck. "Do you think he's got a shot at this opening?"

She shrugged. "These things aren't usually by merit but I'd love for him to get it."

"Over your dad?" I asked, remembering that Judge Reynolds had also been named as a candidate.

"Dad doesn't have a snowball's chance in hell." She shook her head and regarded me with a smile. "I can see by your expression you're not in the loop on legal politics in the state.

Dad's considered radical and unpredictable. The only reason he got his position was because the citizens orchestrated a campaign, making it very clear they wouldn't accept anyone else for the opening. Polefax County is the most liberal in the state, and the voters are loud and active—just like my dad."

"And the rest of the state doesn't approve?" I asked.

"I'm sure some voters in other counties would support him, but he's a bit too out there for most of the state. It is what it is. I'm sure he's been nominated to appease a vocal minority that insisted he be considered for the opening."

I glanced over at Judge Beck. "Honestly now—do you really think Judge Beck has a chance at this appellate court opening?"

She followed my gaze. "Who knows? It'll probably go to the guy who plays golf with one of the judges, or the guy who donated a ton of money to a judge's pet charity. That's how these things go."

I had a hard time being as accepting as Ruby was about that, but there was nothing I could do about the way politics worked in our state and country other than vote and vocally express my opinion.

"Your dad, Judge Beck, and Trent Elliott with SMS&C are candidates. Do you know if anyone else is being considered? Who do you think the forerunner is?" I asked her, curious about the competition that hadn't been mentioned in the news.

I nearly choked at the first name she ticked off on her fingers.

"Well, there's Horace Barnes."

"*What?*" I looked around with a grimace and lowered my voice.

"I know, but the guy's been around forever and in spite of being with a smaller firm in Milford, everyone knows him. Don't worry. This is probably more of an appeasement nomination than anything. Horace is happy and feels loved, and when he doesn't get the position, he can blame his loss on all the not-so-imaginary peers who dislike him."

I nodded. It wasn't that *I* particularly disliked Horace Barnes, but he hardly seemed like the ideal candidate for an appellate court judge.

"Then there's Elaine Stallman. Personally I don't think she's ready for it yet, but she's definitely a lawyer to watch. The nomination will get her some attention, and she'll probably wind up with a federal court position in the next decade. Plus it makes the appellate court judges look good for considering a woman in a field of male candidates."

I looked around the room. "Is she here tonight?"

Ruby shook her head. "Not that I've seen, but this place is packed. There's got to be almost a hundred people crammed into this atrium. I'm dreading the restroom line."

I nodded, thinking that was another reason to not overindulge on the wine. "How about Trent Elliott? He's a lawyer here at SMS&C, isn't he? What are his chances?"

"Better than good. I'm thinking Trent Elliott will get it." She made a face at the name.

"You don't like him?" I asked.

She shrugged. "It's not what I think that matters. He's respected, well connected. He's looking at a partnership at SMS&C if he doesn't get this opening. The guy is moving up the ladder like he was shot out of a rocket."

I frowned thinking a partnership would make this firm SMSC&E. That was a whole lot of letters, but when it came to law firms, I guessed that didn't matter a whole lot.

"There are seven appellate judges weighing in on the nominations, but the final decision is made by the governor." Ruby glanced around the room. "Who I haven't seen tonight either."

I nodded. "We saw Katherine Nguyen when we came in. Maybe she's here in his stead?"

Ruby shrugged. "It could be that he's already made his decision and letting the other judges weigh in is just a courtesy."

A very necessary courtesy, I thought. These judges could become a politician's worst nightmare with their rulings. Not only was it important for the governor to appoint someone he felt would be in agreement with him on matters of law, it was also important that he didn't ruffle the feathers of any of the other appellate court judges in the process. But just as the politicians needed to think about their relationship with the judges, the judges also needed to be aware of their relationship with the politicians. Appellate court positions were for ten years. That mayor a judge snubbed might end up being the governor who decided whether or not to extend his term. Or even who might choose to recommend him to a federal seat.

In the end it was all about politics. It should have bothered me, and in a way it did, but the reality was that networking and schmoozing was a game played in more than this room. As much as he tried to avoid it, Eli had needed to make the rounds with the big hospital donors and the board just as Judge Beck was doing now with the lawyers and other judges.

Maybe Trent Elliott would get the position. Maybe not. Either way, I was here to help Judge Beck advance his career, and possibly pick up a little future business for myself. But right now my wine glass was empty, and I really wanted more of those lobster canapés.

"Want to join me on a quick raid of the buffet table?" I asked Ruby.

She laughed. "Does a duck quack? Heck yeah. And I wouldn't mind another wine either."

I glanced over, but Judge Beck was deep in conversation with Sonny Magoo as well as two other men I hadn't yet met. Not wanting to interrupt him, I headed off with Ruby. I'd track him down later, probably still in the same spot, still talking legalese with the other judges. And if not, well we both had our cell phones with us. It wasn't like we couldn't find each other with a quick text.

CHAPTER 3

*R*uby and I ate and chatted a bit before she headed off to the ladies' room and I made my way back to where I'd last seen Judge Beck. He was no longer there, and I found myself weaving through the crowd searching for someone I'd been introduced to. The room was growing warm, and a good number of the men had removed their jackets, draping them over the scant chairs. I saw Sonny Magoo chatting with the woman in the red dress that Irene had said was Helen Dixon over by the dance floor, and both Judge and Justine Sanchez near the roped-off staircase, but no Judge Beck. In my wanderings, I found myself back by the buffet, dangerously close to those lobster appetizers I was too weak to resist. Hmmm. Maybe I could indulge in one more, then keep looking for Judge Beck.

"Have you had these yet? They're amazing."

I turned to see a petite woman enjoying the lobster canapés with just as much enthusiasm as I'd been doing. She was wearing a high-necked gold gown that flared out mid-calf, making her look like a cross between a raven-haired mermaid and a flamenco dancer. On either side of her, making no effort to appear unobtrusive, were two huge, buff guards.

"Here. You've got to try one." The lieutenant governor extended her plate which must have held half a dozen of the appetizers.

"I think I've already eaten an entire tray of these," I confessed, willing myself not to snatch one off her plate.

"Well, if it makes you feel any better, you're not the only one." She pushed the plate further toward me. "You've got to help me here. If I eat all these, I'll explode out of my dress. Can you imagine the scandal? I'd be internet famous, and not in a good way."

I laughed and took one of the lobster canapés off her plate, popping it into my mouth. She ate one as well, then forced her two guards to finish off the rest as she extended a hand to me.

"I'm Kathrine Nguyen."

"Kay Carrera. It's very nice to meet you, Lieutenant Governor." I should have been awestruck to be at a party actually chatting with one of our state's highest public servants, but I wasn't. Maybe it was the wine or maybe it was the casual and friendly way she'd struck up a conversation with me, but I felt an instant rapport with this woman.

Of course, that's what made a good politician—the ability to chat in a warm and informal manner with your constituents.

We spoke for a bit about the weather, and the upcoming holiday. Then she tilted her head and regarded me thoughtfully.

"I knew your name sounded familiar. Locust Point. Are you the woman who helped find the evidence to charge and convict the mayor on two counts of murder?"

"Yes, although I didn't do it alone." A good bit of my help

came from a ghost, but I wasn't about to confess that bit of information.

"And the Holt Dupree murder." She laughed. "Goodness, I *am* glad to meet you!"

She went on to pepper me with questions about the various murders I'd found myself smack in the middle of this past year while I debated bringing up Judge Beck's nomination and putting forth a plea for her to put a favorable word in with the governor. Ultimately I decided that although the lieutenant governor was probably used to those types of requests, for me to do it felt crass and impolite.

"There you are."

I turned when I heard Judge Beck's voice behind me and got to see the quickly hidden expression of surprise when he saw who I was talking to.

"Judge Beck, have you met our lieutenant governor?" I turned back to face Katherine Nguyen, reaching back to tug the judge forward. "Ms. Nguyen, this is Judge Nathaniel Beck of our county circuit court. I'm his guest this evening."

She reached out to shake his hand. "First, thank you so much for bringing Ms. Carrera tonight. I've had a lovely time speaking with her. Secondly, I do believe you're on the short list of candidates for the appellate court opening?"

The judge's nod was almost a bow. "I do have that honor, Ms. Nguyen. And I couldn't imagine bringing anyone tonight besides Kay."

The informal address…the way he slid his hand around to my lower back…did he realize the implication? Because our lieutenant governor certainly did.

Her eyes twinkled, and she shot me a quick smile before turning again to the judge. "There are very qualified candidates for this opening. I know the governor has a difficult choice ahead of him. I want you to know, Judge Beck, that even if you don't get this position, we are very aware of the work you're doing in Milford and that the governor and I see quite a future ahead of you."

My heart sank as I read between her words and realized Judge Beck would most likely not be getting this opening. His face betrayed nothing, and he carried on short pleasant conversation with Katherine Nguyen before she excused herself, telling the judge how nice it was to meet him in person, and me how much she enjoyed our conversation.

As she walked away flanked by her security guards, I sighed. "I'm sorry. Seems like Trent Elliott is going to end up with the position after all. Which isn't really fair, if you ask me. He's not even a judge. Personally I think someone should serve as a judge for at least a few years before they end up on the appellate court."

He shrugged. "I knew it was a long shot. Honestly, it's probably for the best. I love what I'm doing now. Plus I can go ahead and book that ski vacation and not worry about it impacting a promotion."

"There's another plus." I grinned and waited for him to look down at me with raised eyebrows. "We can enjoy ourselves tonight and not have to spend the evening buttering up politicians, judges, and lawyers."

He laughed. "There's no one else here but politicians, judges, and lawyers—well beside some of their spouses and dates, I guess. Besides, I thought you enjoyed your conversation with our lieutenant governor."

"I did, but that was because we didn't discuss politics and I didn't try to ask her to do anything for me. Or you."

He looked into the crowd where Ms. Nguyen had vanished. "She did hot foot it out of here once she realized I was a candidate for that opening."

True. I guess I wasn't the only one who was getting worn out with the networking and the game of social chess.

"I have to confess that I feel like I've been a bad date,

leaving you on your own while I chat up lawyers and other judges." The judge arched an eyebrow at me. "You're right. This should be fun. And now it can be since I'm clearly as much out of the running as Horace Barnes and Rhett Reynolds."

I smiled. "I didn't mind the work. That's why you're here, *and* why you invited me. Besides I've been busy networking for my own career, and trying to figure out the lay of the land when it comes to the hierarchy of lawyers and judges in the state."

He grimaced. "None of that sounds like a fun evening, and in spite of the need to combine business and pleasure, I'd hoped there would be more pleasure than business tonight."

"It's okay. Really." I waved my wine glass at him. "The food is good. The booze is free. And just in case you're concerned, this is my second glass of wine, unlike Irene O'Donnell who I think has gone through an entire case by now."

Judge Beck looked at my empty glass then over at the bar. "Well at least let me provide you with a fresh glass of wine to carry around and occasionally sip while we find people to have non-business conversations with."

He took the glass from my hand but before he could head for the bar, a pianist joined the quartet and they began a song that filled me with joy. They'd been interspersing holiday tunes with classical music, but this selection was my absolute favorite.

The judge stopped and looked back at me. "'Rhapsody on a Theme of Paganini'?"

"Rachmaninov," I said.

He shoved my empty wine glass at a random passerby, and took my hand. "Will you do me the honor of this dance, Ms. Carrera?"

I managed to execute an old-fashioned curtsy in my slim dress. "The honor would be mine, Judge Beck."

I let him lead me out to the floor, looping the strap of my clutch around my wrist as he turned and pulled me into his arms. My one hand was on his shoulder, the other clasped in his. His free hand snaked around my waist and drew me close enough that I could feel the heat from his body, but not so close that I was actually pressed against him. We moved to the music in a sort of waltz step, him guiding me with the pressure of his hands as we slowly spun around the dance floor.

The sweet cadence of the violins swam through my blood, intoxicating me more than the two glasses of wine I'd consumed. I took a wrong step, then recovered, my thigh brushing against the judge's. He tightened his grip on my waist and I relaxed into him, closing the distance and resting my head against his shoulder.

The dance steps slowed, becoming more of a gentle sway. We both stopped and hesitated for a moment as the music came to an end, the pair of us stepping away as the quartet began to play "It Came Upon A Midnight Clear".

"Thank you," I murmured, suddenly embarrassed and not sure how to process the feelings swimming through me.

"It's one of my favorite songs." His voice was soft, his hand still on my waist as he turned to lead me off the dance floor.

"Mine too." A friend had introduced me to the song in college. I'd never been much into classical music, but this one had lodged itself inside my heart. I couldn't help but stop what I was doing and lose myself in the melody every time I heard it. For me, the song meant romance. It meant love.

And it wasn't lost on me that the whole time I was dancing with Judge Beck and listening to the seductive strains, I never once thought of Eli.

It was like cold water dashed on my happiness. Eli. All those decades of marriage and love. An entire life we'd built together. How could I not think of him? He hadn't even been gone a year and here I was in another man's arms, feeling emotions I had no right to be feeling.

"I...I really should find the ladies' room." It wasn't a lie. I really did need to go after two glasses of wine, and the break would give me a chance to try to figure out what the heck was going on with me, with him, with *us*.

"To the left, past the Christmas tree." The judge pointed, then slid his hand from my waist. "I'll get another wine for you in the meantime."

I'll admit that I fled. Well, I tried not to make it obvious, but my heart pounded up in my throat and I forced my steps to look casual as I moved away, speeding up as I approached the line for the bathroom.

I still stood in line, trying to catch my breath and get control of my emotions. When we hadn't moved in ten minutes, I started to fidget. This was crazy. I was beginning to feel as if I were waiting to use the facilities at a huge outdoor concert venue.

"What the heck is everyone doing in there?" I muttered half to myself, half to the woman behind me.

She shrugged, seeming to be unfazed by the slow-moving line. "Fixing their make-up? Gossiping? Doing lines?"

I glanced across at the men's bathroom, which never seemed to have the same amount of wait time as the women's. Back in college, I would have said 'screw it' and just used the men's, but I didn't think that would fly at a posh event like this, or at my age.

After a few more minutes I gave up, deciding I didn't have to go bad enough to spend half the evening in a bathroom line. Hopefully in an hour or so, when my situation became more urgent, either the line wouldn't be quite as long, or everyone would be drunk enough that no one would notice a sixty-year-old woman in a silk dress barging into the men's.

I stood by the Christmas tree for a moment, trying to see if Judge Beck was still over near the bar when a familiar voice greeted me.

"Almost makes you want to go outside and pee behind a bush, doesn't it?" Justine Sanchez gestured toward the line.

"I should have worn an adult diaper, although I don't think it would do anything for my silhouette in this dress." I ran a hand along my hip, feeling the snug fit of the gown.

"No it wouldn't." Justine shot me an impish grin. "Want to know a secret? Just between you and me, there's a bathroom up on the second floor right off the atrium. It used to be an executive washroom, but they converted it into an office restroom a few years back. I sneak up there when I don't want to spend half an hour doing the pee dance while waiting my turn."

I looked at the roped-off stairs and bored guards with uncertainty. Would they care if I told them where I was going and why? Would they insist on accompanying me? Besides the guards, anyone facing that direction would see me heading up the wide steps into the clearly off-limits area. Although I would welcome a trip to the facilities, my bladder wasn't in such a state that I wanted to risk the embarrassment of being caught going somewhere I shouldn't.

"There's an elevator back behind the staircase," Justine added. "Second floor. Take a left out of the elevator, the first right, then two doors down on the right. You'll see the sign."

I hesitated, inexplicably wanting to ask if she'd come with me. I don't know why. I was perfectly capable of taking an elevator up one flight on my own, and if I was stopped I could simply say that one of the guests told me to use the facilities up there. Yes, women did tend to head to the powder room in pairs, but it wasn't like Justine and I needed to exchange opinions on our dates or borrow feminine hygiene products from each other. Still, I couldn't hold back the odd shiver at the thought of going to that second-floor bathroom alone.

I saw Judge Sanchez beckon to his wife, and that made my fears seem all the more irrational. "Thanks. I'll be down in a few. If you see Judge Beck, let him know I'll be right back."

She smiled and headed toward her husband while I turned in the opposite direction. I made my way around a packed dance floor, trying not to get in the way of couples swaying to Silent Night. Skirting the edge of where the string quartet was playing, I circled around behind the stairs, and did indeed see an elevator too small to be used for moving furniture and other bulky items, but sufficient for possibly three people to use simultaneously. I hit the up button, thinking that there must be a service elevator somewhere in the rear of the building, away from all this marble and gold. Clearly SMS&C preferred their employees and clients take the sweeping staircase at least to the second floor because I got the impression this elevator had been installed as a grudging acquiescence to state and federal disability accessibility laws.

The door opened with a swoosh and I entered, punching the button for the second floor. Within seconds, the doors opened again and I was treated to a breathtaking view of the atrium below from the catwalk that circled the entry area. The acoustics up here were even better than downstairs and I took a second to look down at all the bald and silver heads atop suited bodies. So many men. And it seemed that a large percentage of the women present were here as spouses or plus-ones—even though those I'd spoken with were professional women and often lawyers themselves.

It made me think back to my youth, to when we women

were fighting for equal opportunity in careers, and the amount of amused head-patting we'd received from those who felt our demands were just temporary tantrums of the young—tantrums that would fade once we were married and happily ensconced in motherhood. It made me burn with anger to think that things hadn't changed all that much since the seventies.

I did a quick sweep to make sure no one, especially the guards, was looking up and my way, then quickly made my way along the catwalk hallway and down the corridor. Justine's directions were spot on, and I found the restroom well marked. It was a door out of place in the symmetrical nature of the office placements. I was willing to bet that if I'd taken a tape measure, I would have found each door an exact distance from each other, the ones across the hall staggered so they didn't open across from each other. The offices were clearly large, not the tiny ones I'd seen in our local law firms, or the bullpens of cubicles I'd imagined in a firm of this size. Although I'm sure the bullpen of the lowest-level employees was somewhere else in the building. Probably down next to the boiler room or something.

The room was marked as mixed gender, so I knocked and hesitated a second before turning the handle and opening the door. I wasn't sure if the furnishings were typically opulent, or a remnant of this bathroom's former status as an executive washroom, but one thing was clear. The dove gray walls were not meant to include a heavy splattering of red.

And the cream marble floor tiles were not supposed to have a body lying on them.

CHAPTER 4

I sucked in a breath, nearly jumping out of my skin as the door closed behind me with an audible click. A man. In a tux. Blood everywhere—splashed on the back wall and the full-length mirror. Speckled on the sink, and the louvered door for the toilet area. A pool of red circled around the man, sluggishly oozing outward.

And over his body hovered the faint shadow of a ghost.

I held back on my initial urge to flee, then held back on my secondary urge to go assist the man. Assuming that was his spirit hovering above him, would that mean he was already dead? The slowly expanding pool of blood made me think his heart might still be beating, but as little as I knew about the human body, I was pretty sure that with so much blood loss, the man's heart wouldn't be beating for long. And a wound, or wounds, that produced that sort of injury would be far beyond my ability to help. "Apply pressure" would definitely not do any good.

The only good I could think to do was make a phone call. I fumbled to pull my cell phone from my purse, and dialed.

"Kay? Where are you? Why are you calling me? Did you skip out and take an Uber home or something?"

The warm amusement in Judge Beck's voice instantly snapped me out of my shock. I hadn't realized I'd been in shock, but that was the only explanation I could think of for calling the judge instead of 911.

"I'm upstairs. On the second floor. Second hallway on the right, or maybe left. I don't know. It's a restroom. Justine Sanchez knows where it is." I was whispering for some reason, as if I didn't want the man on the floor to hear.

A chill ran through me as I realized that I might not be alone after all. What if I'd interrupted the murder? What if the killer was hiding in the stall?

Common sense dictated I turn around and get the heck out of the bathroom, but I didn't want to leave the crime scene unattended. Plus I still must have been in shock, because instead of going with my common sense, I walked forward and nudged open the stall door with the edge of my purse.

Whew. Empty. I looked up to make sure the killer wasn't hanging like Spiderman on the ceiling tiles—which he thankfully wasn't.

"What? Are you locked in?" Judge Beck laughed. "Do you need me to come get you out or make excuses to the security guards and our hosts about why you're upstairs in the office areas?"

"No, there's a dead man in the bathroom." I was still whispering as I backed toward the door.

He made a startled noise. "Dead? Overdose? Heart attack? Did you call 911? Are you doing CPR?"

"No. Someone killed him. There's blood everywhere, and I'm sure he's dead by now." The investigative side of my brain started to kick in and I looked around. "I don't see a murder weapon anywhere. I don't remember seeing blood in the hallway either but the killer *must* be covered in blood. Call 911 for me and I'll wait here to make sure the murderer doesn't come back and try to tamper with the body or the evidence. Oh, and after you call, look around and see if anyone has blood splatter on them."

I doubted it. The killer would have either fled, or if they were employed here, they might have gone into their office to hide, or maybe to change out of the bloody clothing. I seemed to recall a lawyer friend telling me once that he always kept a change of clothes in his office in case he pulled an all-nighter and needed to refresh for the morning without taking the time to go home.

Judge Beck told whoever was standing next to him to call 911, then to "Go get Sullivan and tell him someone's died in the second-floor bathroom." I wondered for a moment why he wasn't calling himself, then realized that he didn't want to disconnect our call.

"I'm on my way," he said to me.

Judging from the other sounds over the phone, he seemed to be pushing people out of the way. I heard him say something to the security guards in his authoritative judge-voice, then the sounds of his footsteps on the stairs. I opened the door and peeked out to see him rounding the corner, slowing to a brisk walk as he saw that I was physically fine.

"Be careful," I warned him as he reached the door. "It's not a huge bathroom, and there's a lot of blood. I'm trying to stay out of it."

He squeezed in beside me, his eyes widening. "That *is* a lot of blood."

"But you didn't see any in the hallway though, did you? I'd expect if I bludgeoned someone to death—and I'm assuming here, it could have been a knife but not a gun because I think we would have heard that even over the party and the music. Anyway, the killer should have blood on him. There should have been blood drops in the hallway, right? Or bloody footprints?"

Judge Beck drew in a deep breath. "Kay, you're a very unusual woman, you know that?"

"Yes, I do. Now, about the blood...?"

He shook his head and let out a soft laugh. "I'm not a homicide detective, but as a circuit court judge who has seen plenty of evidence during murder trials, I'd say there should be trace evidence in the hallway. The murderer may have taken his shoes off and wrapped them in something, or been stupid enough to throw them in the trash, but I'm sure he left prints or a drop or two of blood on the doorway, the door handle, or in the hallway."

I felt guilty as I looked behind me at the door. "I grabbed that door handle."

"I'm fairly certain no one will mistake you for the murderer," Judge Beck commented drily.

"In a white silk dress? Hardly. I'm more worried that I may have smudged the only decent fingerprints of the murderer."

There was a sound of a gruff male voice ordering someone to keep the others back. The door opened, nearly flattening the judge and me, and in barged an elderly, wire-thin, bald man in a tux.

The man immediately shouted an expletive, then sent an apologetic glance my way before turning to the judge.

"No one said there was all this blood. I thought someone OD'd or had a heart attack. Who is it?"

"No idea. And I'm not about to turn him over to see," Judge Beck replied. "Kay, this is Charles Sullivan, one of the partners here at SMS&C. Charlie, this is my guest Kay Carrera. She's the one that found the body."

Charlie Sullivan had squatted down and angled himself sideways as he looked at the body. With a grimace and a glance at the floor, he dropped to his hands and knees, lowering his face to within a few inches of the marble.

"Nice to meet you, Ms. Carerra. Well, it would be nice to meet you under any other circumstances. Not to be rude or anything, but why were you up here?"

I felt as if I'd been caught smoking in the bathroom in high school—the off-limits bathroom in the teachers' lounge.

"There was a line downstairs and one of the other guests told me about the restroom." I sent Judge Beck an apologetic wince. "And the elevator behind the stairs."

Charlie made a "harrumph" noise. "Next year we're gonna put locks on this door and rat traps in the hallway. And I'll spring for a few porta potties. No one but employees are supposed to be up here."

"I'm so sorry." I squirmed a bit, wondering if this was going to get me blacklisted from future events, or if my behavior would harm the judge's reputation somehow. I doubted it, given that he'd called the partner of a major law firm by a nickname.

Charlie stood and eyed the sink to wash his hands, obviously trying to decide if washing his hands would compromise the crime scene. "Not that I want anybody stumbling across this kind of thing, but I'm actually grateful, Ms. Carrera. This is an upper-level employee floor and there was a good chance no one would have found this guy until Monday morning."

That was a horrible thought. Surely someone would have noticed him missing and realized that he was last seen at the party here? I was assuming he was a guest due to the fancy attire, but I guess he might have been a burglar trying to look like he fit in.

I frowned at the thought. "Any idea why *he* might have been up here? Or whoever did him in? I doubt someone killed him for using an off-limits bathroom."

Charlie shrugged. "Maybe he was doing someone's wife, or screwed another lawyer over, or lost a case defending a drug lord."

My eyebrows shot up. "A drug lord would lure someone to an upstairs bathroom to kill him with nearly a hundred lawyers and judges plus the lieutenant governor and security guards one floor below? Why not just do a drive-by at his office? Or when he was out shopping?"

"Maybe he was drunk and hit his head on the marble when he passed out. Heck if I know. The police'll figure it out."

I glanced over at Judge Beck, appalled that a senior partner in a major law firm was so blasé about a bloody crime scene in an office bathroom.

"I doubt he came up here because the men's line was too long," Judge Beck chimed in. "I was in and out with only two people ahead of me. There had to be a reason for him to come up here, and it wasn't to use the bathroom."

Well, there *were* a lot of reasons someone might want privacy in a quiet, out-of-the-way bathroom. Maybe the man had an intestinal emergency and didn't want everyone at the party commenting on how some guy blew up the bathroom with toxic waste. Maybe he'd imbibed too much and wanted to throw up the excess alcohol without others listening in. Maybe he was shy, or needed to empty a colostomy bag. But none of those things were a precursor to winding up dead on the floor with blood soaking into the marble.

Perhaps Charlie was right. This could have been a tryst gone wrong. Or someone with a grudge followed the man up here and stabbed him before he could empty his colostomy bag in private. Hopefully the detective that was assigned to this case would quickly get to the bottom of it, because as heartless as it sounded standing here ten feet away from a man who'd most likely died by violent means, I was curious.

I was pretty sure curiosity had never killed any cat. It certainly hadn't killed Taco to date, and I doubted it would kill me. At least I hoped it didn't wind up killing me. I'd had a few close brushes over the last year, and this might be a good time in my life to think about taking it easy and letting the cops do their jobs.

Or not.

We heard what sounded like an army of booted footsteps, along with the clank of what I assumed was a stretcher. Judge Beck looked down the hallway and stepped out to hold the door open.

In no time at all the bathroom was filled with police. The three paramedics in fire department uniforms took one look at the scene and turned it over to the cops. I knew from casual chats with Miles over scones and muffins that dispatch always sent someone from fire and rescue, just in case the caller was wrong and the dead person was not, in fact, dead. But once they'd confirmed there was no need for them, they left. Evidently paramedics' and EMTs' job duties ended when a person was actually dead on the scene, and at that point the police and the coroner's, or M.E.'s office took over.

The police had come well-prepared. One placed little numbered placards around and took photos while another shooed us out of the bathroom and started prepping to take statements. Three uniformed officers hung outside the room with another man in casual clothes, and an aggravated woman who looked like she'd just come from a holiday party of her own. I positioned myself so I could see into the bathroom between the two officers, trying to listen in.

Done with the pictures, the plainclothes officer ushered the fancy-dress woman forward. She took a pair of booties, gloves, and what looked like a plastic rain poncho from a uniformed cop then slipped them on before heading into the room. I watched her feeling a whole lot of sympathy. She must be the poor woman from the M.E.'s office that had gotten yanked out of a formal function to attend a crime scene.

I waved off the woman taking statements and sent her to Charlie Sullivan, hoping he had enough to keep her occupied while I watched. Moving to get a better view, I saw the woman in her plastic poncho survey the scene, bending down to floor-view as Charlie had done. Then she stood and conferred with the uniformed officer who'd been taking photos before walking gingerly into the blood pool with her bootied shoes.

When she turned the body over, I caught my breath. Around his neck, instead of the plain black bow tie the other men were wearing with their tuxes, was one embellished with striped candy canes edged in shiny gold.

It was Rhett Reynolds. *Judge* Rhett Reynolds. I leaned closer into the doorway to better see his face, and confirmed it. Even with all the blood and the horrible head wound I recognized the man. I reached out a hand to Judge Beck's sleeve, suddenly, and probably irrationally, worried for *his* safety.

A judge, murdered. So much for all that security downstairs.

Looks like he was hit with a blunt object to the left temple. I wasn't sure if I knew that from my journalist past, my current detective job, or because I'd played a lot of Clue as a kid and had watched more than my fair share of television mysteries. Either way, I couldn't tell if the blow marring his head had been enough to kill the man, but I was assuming so. What weapon had the murderer used? And where was it? Surely the killer wasn't walking around a law firm in blood-covered clothing with a tire iron or something in his hand.

"Are there any other entrances to the building?" I overheard a police officer ask Charlie.

The lawyer nodded. "There's a service entrance around back that comes in the basement floor. It's locked and alarmed—at least it's supposed to be. There's a service elevator there as well for moving desks and files to the offices, but it requires a key to operate. Because of the high-profile guests we have two guards back there watching that entrance."

"Any access to this floor beyond the staircase from the atrium, the elevator from the atrium, and the service elevator?" the officer asked, scribbling furiously into a pad of paper.

Charlie pursed his lips in thought. "We've got two sets of fire stairs at the east and the west ends of the building, but to get to those someone would need to either come in the service entrance or use the atrium."

Two officers went off with Charlie, no doubt to look at the fire stairs as well as the service elevator and entrance. The medical examiner called out a body temperature of ninety-eight degrees. A hand touched my arm, pulling my attention from the crime scene and to a female officer who smiled apologetically at me. "Mrs. Carrera? You were the one who discovered the body? I'd like to take your preliminary statement while it's all still fresh in your mind."

I let go of Judge Beck's sleeve, unaware that I'd still been holding it. That's when I noticed him regarding me, his brow furrowed with concern.

"Are you all right, Kay? Do you want me to come with you?"

I wasn't sure how "right" I was at the moment, but I forced a smile and shook my head. "I'll be okay. I'm sure they'll want your statement as well. Meet you downstairs when they're all done with us?"

Judge Beck nodded and I turned to follow the officer down the hall and to the elevator. This was going to be a daunting task for them. Unless they found evidence that the guards out back had been negligent or overpowered and the service door had been used, they'd need to consider everyone here attending the party as a potential suspect. If the murderer was at the party, someone may have seen him or her sneaking up the stairs under the rope, or perhaps taking the back elevator.

I glanced over the edge of the railing, counting. Five officers down there were slowly working their way around a very curious group of lawyers and judges. A few glanced up at me and I quickly stepped back, nearly running into the officer I was following.

"We've gotten approval to use the first-floor offices behind the atrium," she said as she pushed the down button for the elevator.

"The insurance company offices?" Or were they CPA offices? I couldn't remember what Judge Beck had said.

"I'm not sure. Someone at the station called and arranged it."

That made sense. They could hardly stuff nearly a hundred high-profile people in formal dress into a bus and haul us all down to the station for questioning, and they would be considering the atrium and the SMS&C floors to be part of the crime scene.

I accompanied the woman into the elevator, then around the edges of the atrium to where another officer was standing by a double glass door. He let us in, and we went into one of the open offices.

"I'm Officer Perkins," the woman told me, as she shut the door and sat across from me. With a smile she pulled a note pad and pen out of her pocket as well as a small recorder. Clicking the recorder on, she stated her name, the date and time, and asked for me to state my name for the record.

"Kay Carrera," I told her. Then I recited my address and my phone number as she wrote.

"Can you tell me what lead to you finding the deceased?" She smiled again, and I wondered if they included "reassuring witnesses" in police academy training.

I told her about the lines downstairs for the ladies' room, that Justine Sanchez had clued me in on the bathroom upstairs and the elevator, then I told her exactly what I'd observed walking to and entering the restroom where I'd found the bloody body.

I left out the part about the ghost. He'd remained upstairs hovering over the body, but this wasn't my first time discovering a murder victim, and I had a strong feeling that ghost was going to be following me home—then following me around until I brought his killer to justice.

"I'm sorry, what?" I winced, realizing that Officer Perkins had been asking me a question.

She frowned. "How many people at the party know about this upstairs bathroom?"

I shrugged. "Well, the lawyers who work here probably know about it as well as people who might have visited the lawyers working on the second floor. Beyond that, I don't know. The big question is why Judge Reynolds was up there. The line for the men's was pretty short. So I'm assuming he had a specific reason for going upstairs. Maybe someone followed him. Or maybe someone went up with him for a private conversation or a tryst, although why they'd want to do that in a restroom, I don't know."

Officer Perkins had blinked in surprise midway through my speech. "You knew the decedent? I mean, you recognized him?"

"I don't know him very well, but I did recognize him even

if I hadn't noticed his holiday-themed bowtie. I only met Judge Reynolds tonight. Although I spoke with his daughter a bit, I didn't speak directly with him that I recall. But I did recognize him as the deceased man on the bathroom floor."

I don't know why I held back the bit about my conversation with Irene O'Donnell. Given our conversation, I'd think her to be a suspect, but in spite of that, I was pretty sure she hadn't killed Judge Reynolds. She *did* have motive. As an employee here, she most likely knew the existence of the second-floor bathroom. But she had been drunk off her butt and certainly not in any position to sneak upstairs or to the elevator unnoticed. Then there was the pesky matter of the weapon. Until I knew what it was, I couldn't definitively rule Irene out, but she didn't seem the premeditated type, and I couldn't see her getting the upper hand against a sober Judge Reynolds in a fight, even if she'd managed to lug a baseball bat or tire iron through the party and upstairs unnoticed.

Actually no one would have been able to. What could have been the murder weapon? My mind immediately drifted to all sorts of odd items that might fit the bill. A marble rolling pin that had been used as a restroom decoration? A metal bat that an employee had left lying in the hallway from Friday softball practice in the middle of December? A music stand from the string quartet? Surely they would have noticed one missing after their short break.

"I'm sorry, what?" Drat. For the second time I'd completely missed what Officer Perkins had asked. She sighed, giving me a long-suffering look.

"Tell me about your conversation with the decedent's daughter."

I told her we'd mostly discussed the viability of the appellate court candidates, including her father.

Officer Perkins blinked and looked up at me with wide eyes. "He was nominated for the opening? Judge Reynolds?"

I nodded and let her know the other candidates as she made notes.

"Did any of them have a problem with Judge Reynolds?"

I lifted my palms. "I really don't know. I don't exactly run in these social circles. I know a few of the judges, lawyers, and officers from my town and my county, but most of these people I've only just met tonight. I *can* say that I didn't witness any altercations, and I'm pretty sure security would have been on top of it if there had been any."

Officer Perkins made a few notes, and I thought about the other candidates. Horace Barnes was just as vocal as Judge Reynolds, although at the opposite end of the political spectrum. I couldn't see Horace getting worked up enough to bludgeon someone to death, though. Then there was Trent Elliott, who I knew nothing about other than he was most likely the front-runner. Since he worked here, he probably knew about the upstairs restroom, but I couldn't think of a reason he'd have to kill Rhett Reynolds. Judge Beck certainly hadn't killed the man. That left Elaine Stallman, the sole female candidate, but I didn't even think she'd attended tonight, let alone had any motive to kill Reynolds.

But Irene O'Donnell... As unlikely a suspect as I thought her to be, she seemed to have both motive and opportunity. Oh, and I'd almost forgotten the spurned lover Helen Dixon —as well as her ex-husband who was an appellate court judge and had to be hating that the man who'd cuckolded him was a candidate to serve beside him at the appellate court.

Most likely there would end up being a dozen other suspects as well—ones that I was completely unaware of. I'm sure there were other lawyers like Irene who'd run afoul of Judge Reynolds' rulings as well as the families and friends of those who'd stood before his bench. Heck, maybe there was another spurned lover or two out there who Helen Dixon had replaced and who wanted to stick a knife in Judge Reynolds or slam him upside the head with something heavy in a quiet second-floor bathroom.

"Oh no! Has anyone told his daughter, Ruby?" I asked Officer Perkins. I'd liked the woman and the affection between her and her father was apparent. How horrible that Ruby's father had been murdered.

The citizens in his county would grieve as well. From what Ruby said, they'd demand justice. This homicide was likely to blow up into a political nightmare. The longer it took the police to find the murderer, the more citizens who loved and supported Judge Reynolds would start their own witch hunts. And a county of vocal and active voters who were especially motivated to grab torches and pitchforks might stir someone into vigilante justice.

That, we did not need.

CHAPTER 5

*S*omeone *had* told Ruby Reynolds. I knew this because I found her across the street at the bar, crying.

Officer Perkins had wrapped up our interview, escorted me to collect my wrap, then escorted me straight to the door where several officers waited until I left, then locked the door behind me. I stood for a few seconds shivering on the steps and wondering what I was supposed to do. Judge Beck had the valet ticket for the SUV. I hadn't memorized the license plate, so there was no sense in me trying to bribe the valets into bringing it around for me without the ticket. I contemplated calling an Uber as the judge had jokingly thought I'd done earlier, but saw that there was a little pub across the street open and decided two glasses of wine wasn't nearly enough for what I'd gone through tonight.

I darted across the wide street, wincing at what the heavily salted road was doing to my nice leather shoes. Wrestling open the heavy door to the pub, I paused a moment to let my eyes adjust to the dim light, and immediately saw Ruby at the bar.

The only other people in the pub were a couple in close, intimate conversation at a back table, and a thin man cradling a pint, his eyes fixed on whatever sport seemed to be playing on the bar's television screen.

I sat down beside Ruby and waved to the bartender, ordering myself a beer.

She glanced over at me, her mascara smeared and her eyes red. "Did you hear what happened?"

I nodded, not sure if it would do any good to tell her I was the one who'd found him. "Yes. I'm gathering the police already spoke to you?"

She stared down at her beer. "I wondered what the heck was going on when dozens of uniformed officers started pouring into the place. When the police chief got up on stage and told us all that they were going to need to speak to each of us individually, that's when I started worrying about why I hadn't seen Dad in a while."

I didn't know what to do so I reached over and patted her hand, blinking in surprise when she gripped my fingers in hers.

"Usually they interview the bigwigs first so they don't go ballistic and raise a fuss, but that entire party was bigwigs. Well, most of the party. When they came and got me first, I felt like I was going to throw up. Somehow I just knew. They asked me if anyone at the party had argued with Dad, if anyone held a grudge against him. They wanted to know who was the last person I'd seen talking to him, as well as who I'd been with the last few hours."

I sucked in a breath. "Surely they didn't think *you* did it?"

She shrugged. "Maybe they wanted to see if I would verify anyone's alibi. After they were done, they offered to give me a ride home since they said they'd need to process Dad's car for possible evidence. I was so numb and confused. How could I go home when Dad's body was still there? It would be like I was leaving him. And I guess a part of me didn't believe it. So I told them I didn't need a ride, got my coat, and came over here. I sat by the front window so I could see if he walked out, if they were lying, but after a while it kind of sunk in."

I looked out the window at the line of police cars, the officers guarding the cordoned-off area, the occasional guest leaving the party, stumbling down the stairs in shock with their valet ticket in hand.

"He's really dead, isn't he?" she whispered.

I gave her hand a gentle squeeze. "Ruby, I'm so sorry. Yes, your father died."

"Murdered." She drained the remaining beer in her glass and motioned for another. "If he'd just had a sudden heart attack, or a freak accident, I think I could cope, but murdered…. Actually no, it's not the way he died, it's the suddenness of it that feels like someone stabbed me in the chest. I was just talking to him a few hours ago. He was warm and alive and laughing. And now he's gone."

There was such a rawness to her voice that my heart twisted. "I too lost someone I dearly loved this year. I know sympathy doesn't do anything to help the pain of grief, but I'm so sorry for your loss, Ruby. So very sorry."

She began to cry once more, this time silent tears that rolled down her face as her chest shook. "He's gone. He was the most important person in my life. He was the reason I went into law, the reason I dedicated my career to helping those who needed justice and couldn't always afford it. Growing up, he was the only stable parent I had. He was my rock, my father, and he's gone. I'll never see him again. I'll never get a text from him late at night, meet him for coffee first thing in the morning, have that ridiculously horrible vegan Thanksgiving dinner with him. I'll never see him again. Never."

I got the feeling that expressions of faith and assurances of a life after death wouldn't be appropriate. Not everyone was Christian, not everyone was all that religious, and not everyone believed in an afterlife. So instead of the expression of sympathy and hope I might have given at a church funeral, I reached out to hug her tight, letting her cry on my shoulder as I rubbed her back.

Finally she sat back, wiping her eyes on a bar napkin and smearing her make-up even more. There was a full pint in front of her, and she lifted it in the air. "To Dad. He was the most honorable man I ever knew. I hope I can follow in his footsteps and make him proud."

I was pretty sure Rhett Reynolds *was* proud of his daughter, but I clinked her glass with mine and echoed "To your father."

We sipped our beer in silence for a moment, then Ruby turned to me. "Can I ask who you lost? If that's too personal, I understand. I just wondered who you'd loved and lost this year."

"Eli. My husband." I told her about the day we'd met, the day he'd proposed. I told her about buying the big Victorian house in Locust Point and how we'd loved rehabbing it and making friends with the neighbors.

I told her about the accident, how things had changed as well as the moments of joy we continued to share together. My life with Eli had been a huge bouquet of those joyful moments, not at all tarnished by the little bumps that happen in even the most loving of marriages.

"I'm sorry for your loss, but it sounds as if you had a wonderful life together."

I nodded. "We did, but I'm only sixty. I've got a whole second life ahead of me without Eli, and I owe it to me as well as him to live...live it the best I can."

I'd almost said "to live and love again". I glanced across

the street, thinking of Judge Beck and wondering how much longer he'd be inside.

"Does it still hurt to think of him? Your husband, I mean?" Ruby asked.

"Some days it hurts. Sometimes I remember the life we shared and I don't think at all about his death, just gratitude that I spent so much of my life by his side. I believe the pain will continue to ease with time, but I'm sure there will always be moments where I remember something special the two of us did, and the ache will come back just as strong."

She nodded, then took another sip of her beer. "I wish I knew more. The police wouldn't tell me what happened to him or even where he was. Did someone shoot him? Poison him? I keep thinking all of these horrible things."

I took a few breaths, wondering again if I should tell her or not. Finally I decided that in her place, I'd want to know.

"I...I'm actually the one who found him, Ruby." I shut my eyes, envisioning once more the man on the restroom floor, the spreading pool of blood, the red splattered against the back wall and the full-length mirror. He must have been killed right before I'd gotten there. Maybe if I'd been just a few minutes earlier—although if I'd been a few minutes earlier there might have been two corpses on the floor of that restroom.

Ruby turned to face me with a startled expression. "You found him? Oh my God, Kay! That must have been so horrible for you. Can you tell me what happened? Where did you find him? What happened to him?"

I might have been about to mess up a police investigation, but Officer Perkins hadn't told me to keep quiet about anything. Besides, Ruby was his *daughter*. She deserved to know.

"The line to the women's room was ridiculous and I had to use the facilities. One of the ladies told me there was an elevator in the back of the atrium that I could take to the second floor, and that there was a restroom up there. When I went in, I saw your father on the floor. So I called…for help."

Now that the shock of the event was starting to recede, I was embarrassed that my first call had been to Judge Beck and not the police. I was a capable independent woman. There was no reason for me to reach out to a man to help me like some seventies' romance heroine.

But I knew if I rewound time, I'd make the same decision. There was something about Judge Beck that made me want to reach out to him when bad things happened. Maybe it was because so many evenings we'd talked about my work and his work. Maybe it was how significant he and his children had become to me. Maybe it was because he was smart, capable, strong, and level-headed. I'd come to lean on him the same way I'd done with Eli. As a partner, an equal. As someone who clicked like a puzzle piece in my life, who worked with me as if we were two halves of a whole. Was it wrong to turn to a friend when a crisis occurred? Daisy and I did the same for each other, and Judge Beck had become just as important to me as my best friend.

More, if I were completely honest with myself.

"What happened to my father?" Ruby's voice was horrified whisper.

I wasn't about to give her the gory details, especially not when she was still in shock over her father's sudden loss. "The medical examiner will know better than me. I'm sure they'll let you know as soon as they have a cause of death."

Ruby stared at her beer for a moment. "But they knew it was murder? Why would someone do that to him?"

I sighed and stared at my own drink, wondering if another beer was a good idea or not. "I don't know. Maybe he surprised someone doing a criminal act. Maybe someone who was angry at him ambushed him in the restroom.

Maybe he was meeting someone up there and they didn't like what he said. The police will figure it out and catch whoever did this."

Her shoulders stiffened. "Helen. She couldn't believe it was over. She'd left her husband of twenty years for Dad, left everything for him, and he was breaking up with her. He told me yesterday it was over between them, but Helen didn't seem to be accepting that. He was worried that she'd make a scene tonight. I was kind of surprised she didn't. Actually she was cool and totally ignored him from what I saw, but maybe she saw him going upstairs and snuck up to take her revenge...."

"But why would he have been using the upstairs bathroom?" I asked. "The line for the men's downstairs wasn't long. There was no reason for him to go up there unless he was either meeting someone, or looking for something, or...I don't know."

"What in the world would he be looking for in an upstairs bathroom, though?" Ruby asked.

"Maybe he wasn't looking for something in the bathroom," I mused. "Maybe he was looking for something in one of the offices and he heard someone coming and hid in the bathroom."

She shook her head. "He's a judge, not a private investigator. Plus I'm pretty sure those offices are all locked. Dad was pretty radical, but I don't think he would have risked a breaking and entering charge to steal something from a locked office."

Perhaps not, but there were some things serious enough to make anyone cross the line and risk their career over.

"So let's talk about the good times you and your father had. You said you really admired him. What were the issues that he was passionate about? The things you loved most about him?"

Ruby smiled, clearly happy to think of something besides her father's murder. "He believed that almost everyone deserved a chance at redemption, but that they had to pay the price for their crime first. He was big on consistent sentencing, regardless of whether the accused had a high-priced attorney, glowing references, or gave a stirring speech about how they'd learned their lesson."

I nodded, thinking of Irene O'Donnell's frustration about her DWI clients.

"He was a stickler for ethics. Anything that hinted at a conflict of interest, people paying others off, or swapping favors incensed him. He truly felt that justice should be blind and hated that politics so often intersected with the judicial system."

"Sounds like someone who might have upset a lot of people in high places," I murmured.

Ruby shrugged. "Not really. The county locals adored him, police and mayor included. Most people at the state level just considered him eccentric. Yes, he was vocal about corruption in law enforcement, and he ruffled feathers, but he worked for general reform and didn't target anyone in particular. Besides, it's not like anything he said or did threatened anyone's career way out in Polefax County like we are."

Except for Irene O'Donnell.

"Well, except for Irene O'Donnell," Ruby said, as if she were reading my mind.

"She was pretty drunk when I talked to her earlier," I commented.

"Sometimes alcohol makes people even more angry, and washes away any self-control they might normally have. Plus drunk people can still shoot a gun. Or stab someone."

I kept my mouth firmly shut, knowing the police wouldn't be happy if I mentioned a possible cause of death.

"Helen wasn't drunk," she added. "Her husband either. You know Judge Dixon used to work in that building, although that was probably almost twenty years ago."

I blinked in surprise, trying to wrestle my brain around that fact. How many of the attendees used to work in the building or currently did? Judge Dixon. Irene O'Donnell. Trent Elliott. Even if they didn't work here, how many lawyers, judges, and politicians had been in and out of the building, meeting with the lawyers of SMS&C? Or whatever other companies were on the other floors?

My phone buzzed and I looked down to see a text from Judge Beck.

Where are you? They said you'd left, but I have the ticket for the car.

I looked over at Ruby, before I responded.

Across the street at the pub. Ruby is here—Judge Reynolds' daughter. She doesn't have a way home. Can we give her a ride?

I made a quick motion telling the bartender to give us the check. My phone buzzed again.

The police didn't arrange for her to have a ride? Where does she live?

Polefax County meant she could be an hour or two west of Locust Point. It wasn't fair to ask the judge to drive four additional hours when he had kids at home waiting for him. But still, I felt terrible for the woman, and she was stuck here without a car.

"Where do you live?" I asked Ruby. "Can I call you an Uber or arrange for a car service to take you home? Do you have friends to stay with you tonight? Someone you can call? I really don't think you should be alone tonight."

"Bridgeville," she replied, telling me the address. "It's kinda late for me to call any friends. I've got a dog though, so I won't be alone tonight."

Bridgeville, I texted. *If it's too late or that's too far, I can arrange for an Uber or something. Or I can offer her a room at our house, if that's okay. Although she's got a dog, and the poor thing probably needs to be let out.*

That was a super long text, but I was blaming it on my frazzled nerves.

Ruby downed her beer. I frowned, worrying about sending her home alone with a car service after the shock she'd had. Would they walk her to the door? What if they ended up being some kind of creep that took advantage of a lone woman? I looked at my phone, thinking that if Judge Beck said he couldn't give her a ride, I might have to go home with her, then take a taxi or Uber home in the morning myself.

Yes, of course we can take her home.

I felt a wave of relief. I'd just met this woman and I hadn't been looking forward to spending the night in an unfamiliar house. I was glad that we'd be giving her a ride to her house, making sure she got in safely with her dog and a supply of water and aspirin. I'd call her tomorrow morning and make sure she was okay and my good Samaritan duty would be done for the week.

"Judge Beck and I can give you a ride home," I told Ruby. "I'll ask him to pull the SUV around for us. Do you have your coat?"

Ruby twisted around on her barstool, nearly falling off it. "It's here. And thank you, but I don't want to be a bother. Maybe I can just get a hotel or something, except Dolly... I could call Jessica next door and see if she can take care of her. She's got a key for emergencies."

"It's no trouble, really," I reassured her. "I think it would be better for you to be in your own home tonight surrounded by comforting familiarity and having Dolly by your side."

Her eyes glistened again with tears. "Thank you. I'm so

grateful. I don't want to inconvenience you and Judge Beck, but it would be nice to be in my own home tonight."

We sat in silence as we waited. I kept an eye out the front window for Judge Beck's SUV, and paid the bill after asking the bartender for three bottles of water to go. I'd just finished signing the credit card receipt when I saw the black SUV pull up front.

"Our ride is here." I reached out a hand to grip Ruby's arm as she slid off the stool onto unsteady feet. Grabbing her coat, I helped her into it before putting on my own, then walked beside her as we made our way to the door.

Judge Beck had put the emergency flashers on his car that was sitting in a fire lane. He hopped out when he saw us, opening both the front and back passenger doors, and taking Ruby's arm to help her into the vehicle. He said a few soft words of condolence, then handed her one of the waters and spread a blanket across her lap.

I was already in the car by the time he'd turned to me, so he closed both doors and walked around to the driver's side, unbuttoning the jacket of his tux and loosening his tie as he climbed in. I handed him one of the waters, and he smiled his thanks, negotiating the SUV out into the traffic.

As we merged onto the highway, I peeked into the back seat to see Ruby sound asleep, her head against the window, the bottle of water unopened in her lap.

"Thank you for this," I whispered to Judge Beck.

"I didn't always agree with Reynolds, but he was a man of strong ethics, and I respect that. It's the least I can do to make sure his daughter arrives home safely."

I looked over at his profile, shadowed and lit only by the gold of the dashboard instrument lights and the occasional overhead ones on the highway. Something in my chest tightened, making me catch my breath.

"I wonder what happened to him." I settled back in the

heated seats, adjusting the vents so the warm air slid over me. "Who hated him so much to do that? And why was he in that upstairs bathroom?"

"Reynolds probably had as many people who hated him as loved him." The judge glanced in the rearview mirror and continued. "Besides his ex-wife, he never had a relationship that lasted more than a few months. Helen Dixon lasted the longest, but I think that was because she was still married for a good bit of their affair."

My shock must have shown on my face because Judge Beck chuckled. "I don't believe he was a Lothario or anything, I just think Reynolds' passion burned hot and fast. He fell hard without really knowing the object of his affection, and once the fire banked down to glowing embers, he realized he'd made a mistake."

Call me old fashioned, but that bothered me. And it definitely bothered me that he'd had an affair with a married woman. Of course, Helen Dixon was even more to blame in that relationship since she was the one breaking her marriage vows.

"Do you think Helen could have killed him?" I asked.

The judge shrugged. "Maybe. I've seen enough heat-of-passion murders in my courtroom. Maybe he was dancing or flirting with someone at the party and Helen just snapped."

"How about Irene O'Donnell?"

He glanced over at me, his expression amused. "You sure did learn a lot in one evening. Irene's a shark, worried about her win ratios and billable hours. She wants partner and Reynolds' rulings were definitely not helping that happen. I doubt she'd sink to murder, though."

"Even if she were really drunk?" I asked.

He shot me another look. "What do you know?"

I squirmed. "She was plowed. We were at the bar and she told me that she wanted to hire me to dig up dirt on Judge

Reynolds, to either get him unseated or possibly to blackmail him."

The judge laughed at that. "There's no blackmailing Reynolds. If there was anything in his past that came to light, then he'd admit it and take his lumps. And those residents in his county wouldn't vote him out for anything. He could have run naked through the streets smoking a bong and they would have cheered for him."

"But did Irene know that?" I asked.

"Once she sobered up, she would have realized it." Judge Beck shook his head. "And I can't see her murdering him. Yes, he was hindering her career goals, but it was just a delay. She'd be better off biding her time and getting reassigned to a different county once she got some seniority."

I didn't want to bring up Judge Dixon and a possible jealousy/revenge motive. It felt unseemly to accuse the man who might one day end up working side-by-side with Judge Beck, so instead I went another direction.

"Do you think one of the other candidates for the appellate court position did it?"

Judge Beck chuckled. "Like me? Convinced I'd never win on my own merit, I decided to clear the field starting with Reynolds."

I swatted at him. "Not you! I mean one of the other candidates."

"This probably sounds arrogant, but Reynolds was never a viable candidate. He wasn't even close to a front-runner for the position. No one would gain from having him dead."

I thought back on what I'd heard at the party and realized that Judge Beck was right. Barnes was being nominated because he was a well-known, nearly retired lawyer. Reynolds was being considered to appease his vocal constituents. The three main candidates in this race were Stallman, Elliott, and Judge Beck, and from what the lieutenant governor had hinted at, Judge Beck wasn't anywhere near the top of that list of three.

Clearly there were a lot of things I didn't know about Judge Rhett Reynolds' life. The police would be the ones to solve this crime, not me. I'd probably read about an arrest in the papers a few months from now, and it would end up being someone he'd sent away looking for revenge, or an old girlfriend from the past. I was curious though, and when I got curious I had a hard time letting go of something. I guess it was the former journalist in me who always wanted to get the story, to get to the bottom of something, to scoop the competition.

I relaxed and sipped my water. It began to snow and Judge Beck switched on the wipers. Their rhythmic whoosh and the spiraling tunnel of snow lit up by the headlights as we drove down the highway mesmerized me. I must have dozed off, because the next thing I remember was the SUV slowing to a stop in front of a split-level brick ranch house with a fenced-in yard.

"I'm so sorry," I said rubbing my eyes and probably smearing mascara all over my face. "What terrible company I am. You had to drive the whole way with two sleeping women."

"It's fine. The quiet gave me time to think about some things. I am hoping that we can get Ruby up and in her house without having to carry her though. And if someone has to retrieve her keys from her purse, it's got to be you. I know better than to ever go into a woman's purse."

"They're always full of mousetraps and sanitary prod-ucts," I teased. "It's good for men to be cautious of such things."

Thankfully Ruby began to stir in the back seat, muttering something about being home already. She blinked open her eyes and as she took in Judge Beck and I, grief creased her face.

"I'll walk you inside," I told her.

"We'll both walk you inside," the judge insisted. I'd offered out of polite kindness, but at the tense note in Judge Beck's voice, I realized something else. This woman's father had been murdered, and we didn't know why or who had done it. For all we knew, there could be someone waiting inside to attack Ruby as well.

Judge Beck put the SUV in park, and left it running, stepping out and surveying the house as I made sure Ruby could stand and walk. The snow had left several inches of light fluffy flakes that reminded me of old-fashioned laundry powder. Our breath billowed in the cold air, and I shivered even in my wrap. The sleep seemed to have cleared most of the beers from Ruby's head, and she made her way to the front door under her own steam, the judge and I following.

There were no other tracks in the snow but ours. As we neared the door, a loud, frantic barking greeted us. Ruby fumbled with her keys, unlocking both the door and a deadbolt before pushing it open.

A dog danced out to greet us. It had the face of a pug, fur like a wire-haired terrier, and the body of a corgi. A whiplike tail beat against our legs and she gave the judge and I an enthusiastic sniff before returning to Ruby.

"Settle down, Dolly." She bent down and hugged the dog, then stood and flicked on the lights in the house."

"Does everything look in order?" Judge Beck asked her.

She nodded. "Yes. And Dolly would have let me know if there was someone else here. She's not much in the way of a guard dog, but there's no way anyone could hide from her."

I dug a card out of my purse and handed it to her. "Can you call me tomorrow morning? Just to let me know everything is okay? I worry leaving you home alone tonight."

Dolly ran off to pee a yellow spot in the snow while Ruby eyed the card. "I'll be okay. I'm kinda numb right now, and tired. I'll just curl up with Dolly and sleep, but I promise to call you in the morning."

"If I can do anything to help, let me know," I urged.

Dolly ran back on the porch, shook the snow off herself, then trotted inside. Ruby backed in the doorway, her hand on the knob. "I will. Thank you again for the ride home. I really appreciate it."

Judge Beck and I said our goodbyes then made our way down the snowy walk, the judge taking my arm as I slid a little in my heels.

"I'm sure this is bringing back some terrible memories for you," the judge mentioned.

For a moment I'd thought of all the murder victims I'd discovered over the last nine months. That party planner. The man across the street. The football star. The author. Was I becoming numb to all this, because although finding Rhett Reynolds in the second-floor bathroom had been horribly shocking, it hadn't particularly brought on any nightmarish memories of other murder victims I'd come across this year.

"It's not that long ago that you lost Eli," Judge Beck added.

I felt a stab of guilt that I'd misunderstood him, thinking he meant memories of a grisly discovery and not grief.

"It's different," I told him as he opened the passenger door for me. "Eli didn't die violently, and in a way I'd been partially grieving him for the last ten years." Memories flooded me, as Judge Beck closed the door and walked around to climb in the driver's side. "The day Eli died…"

The judge started the car and pulled out onto the road. "Go on."

I took a breath. "The day he died seemed normal, just like any other day. He had a bit of weakness in his left side, but he'd been unable to walk and had problems with fine and gross motor skills since the accident, so I didn't really think much about it. It wasn't until later that I got concerned. I made a doctor's appointment for the next day, but by dinner…he started talking gibberish and slurring his words. Eli had cognitive impairments from the accident, but not like this, and these things just don't come out of nowhere ten years after an accident. I called 911, and by the time the ambulance arrived, I was in a state of panic."

Judge Beck reached out to grip my hand, his gaze straight ahead as he guided the SUV out onto the main road.

I took a deep breath and let it out. "I knew it was bad from the way the EMTs were racing around. I rode with them to the hospital then waited while they frantically worked on him."

He squeezed my hand. "But he didn't make it?"

I looked out my window at the fields of freshly fallen snow. "He was on life support with no brain activity. Eli had medical directives, but they'd kept them on to give me time to say goodbye. I'd said goodbye so many times before— when he'd first had the accident, when there'd been terrifying complications in the hospital, that time he'd fallen trying to get into his wheelchair himself and hit his head on the corner of the bed. This time seemed easier. It seemed somehow right. From our first date I felt as if he was my soul mate, if you believe in that sort of thing. And although the accident changed him, I still loved him. It was a different kind of love, because in a way he was a different person, but I loved him."

I felt Judge Beck tense, and we were silent until he pulled onto the highway.

"You've had two terrible losses, Kay," he commented quietly. "The accident, and Eli's death. Nothing in my life is comparable, so it feels disingenuous for me to claim to know how you felt. Both my parents are still alive. And my divorce is hardly comparable to a horrible accident or losing a spouse."

Now it was me squeezing his hand. "Your divorce is a different sort of pain. And although I haven't experienced that, I absolutely sympathize with what you're going through."

He let out a soft laugh and shook his head. "It feels self-indulgent to compare what I'm going through to what you have. Especially the accident. That morning after you came home from witnessing Holt's accident, and told me about Eli's… I can't imagine how horrible that was for you. To love someone so, and to get that call in the morning. To go to the hospital, and not be sure if they were going to make it or not."

Eli's and my marriage hadn't been a fairy tale. There had been arguments. There had been times when both of us had considered walking out. But ultimately we'd put in the hard work to stitch our lives together. I didn't want to pass judgement on those who *hadn't* made it work—especially Judge Beck and Heather. He'd confided in me the issues they'd faced, and there was no villain in that story, just two people who'd grown to want something different.

Then I remembered the terror of that early morning call, the frantic drive to the hospital, the tsunami of emotions as I waited see whether Eli would make it or not. The doctors had done all they could do. I'd stood there, staring at my husband, my beloved, wanting to somehow reverse time, or wake up from what must surely have been a nightmare.

"I know you're a woman of faith," Judge Beck commented. "I'm sure your prayers helped Eli pull through after the accident."

My mind flashed back to ten years ago, and I held onto the judge's hand as if it were a lifeline.

"I didn't pray," I confessed, feeling as if I needed to be

completely honest, as if the dimly lit interior of the SUV was some sort of sanctuary.

Did not praying during the most traumatic moment of my life make me a bad person? My husband had been in a hospital bed barely visible under all the tubes and monitors, not expected to last the night. I should have prayed, but I hadn't.

I forced myself to look out at the wet, salted highway and not at Judge Beck. "I didn't pray. I turned into some sort of Valkyrie. I stood at the end of Eli's bed and envisioned myself facing down the Grim Reaper himself, telling him that he was *not* going to take my husband from me."

It sounded weird, but that's pretty much what I felt had happened. Everyone was grieving. Everyone was praying. But in the midst of all that, I'd grown strong, powerful, determined. If a skeletal man with a scythe had shown up at the hospital that night, I truly think I would have beat him down with an IV stand. Odd as it sounded, that night I felt that somehow, by the strength of my will alone, I could hold Death at bay.

But strength like that doesn't last. Weeks, months, years later I was caring for a man who wasn't really Eli. He was a man who I'd come to love over the ten years we'd had together, but he wasn't the Eli I'd married. Maybe Death *had* won in that hospital room. Maybe when I wasn't looking, the Grim Reaper had stolen away my husband and left me with only echoes of the man I'd loved.

I looked over and saw a hint of wistfulness in Judge Beck's eyes as he glanced at me. "I always wanted that," he said. "I know it sounds twisted but I always wanted someone who would love me so much that they'd face down Death, that they'd be strong when I couldn't be. I wanted someone who would be by my bedside if the worst happened. I still want that. I want that and I want to be that for someone else. I thought I had that with Heather, but I guess not."

I'd cried so much in the past few months—cried for Eli, cried for myself, cried for a past that was gone and a future I feared. Now I wanted to cry again, but this time for Judge Beck.

Instead I squeezed his hand. "That kind of love isn't exclusive to a husband and wife, you know. That very same love can come from a parent, a child, or even your dearest friends. I'd like to think that you'll heal and love again, but don't discount the precious gift of love from family and friends. I know that if it were me in that hospital bed, Daisy would wrestle Death to the ground for me."

Words that were meant to make him felt better, surprisingly made *me* feel better. I was a widow. My parents had passed. I had no brothers or sisters or children. Yet I had friends who I could count on—friends who would drop everything, and indeed wrestle Death to the ground if need be.

The judge chuckled. "I can see that. And I am pretty sure Daisy would win that fight, hands down."

"Madison and Henry would do the same for you," I told him. "Those kids adore you. When you're old and drinking prune juice and the Grim Reaper shows up, Madison and Henry will be there for you, battling on your behalf so you'll have another year to spoil your grandkids. Or great grandkids."

He released my hand to hit the button for four-wheel-drive as the snow began to come down again. "I'll admit that's comforting, but I always saw myself growing old with my wife. Call me old fashioned, but I'd expected marriage to last until death did us part."

"Sometimes God doesn't give you the life you envisioned," I commented. "I believe the key is to do the best with the life you've been given. Every day, every year is a precious gift, and it's up to us to value and cherish each of those days and years."

We drove for a few moments in silence, then he reached down again and took my hand in his. "I believe in that too, Kay. There *are* times when I'm bitter that my life didn't turn out as I'd planned, but increasingly I believe the best moments of my life are before me."

The snow pelted the windshield, and I thought about his words. He was young. He had two amazing children. He had a career he loved. He was making a difference in this world as a man, as a father, and as a judge. I was no psychic, but I honestly felt there could be nothing but success and happiness in his future.

And mine? I searched my heart and felt a sense of peace, of comfort, of strange exhilaration that I hadn't experienced in over a decade. Maybe there were amazing things in my future as well.

And maybe, just maybe, our futures would be down the same path.

CHAPTER 6

"*K*ay. Wake up."

I blinked my eyes open and saw a familiar sight before me. My garage. To my right, my house. The car was still warm but with a creeping chill that told me it had recently been turned off.

Judge Beck leaned over to rub my shoulder. "You were really sleeping hard. I thought about scooping you up and carrying you inside, but I'm not exactly a body builder and I had a horrible vision of me dropping you head-first onto the pavement, or falling backwards down the stairs with you in my arms, or being unable to get the door open while carrying you, or smashing your head against the door jamb as I tried to walk into the house."

I started to laugh. "I think I can make it inside myself if you've got your keys ready." I eyed the snow on my walk. "Although I wouldn't object to a steadying arm to keep me from going down on my butt while walking through the snow in high heels."

"Stay where you are."

I shivered as the cold air blew in when Judge Beck opened the door. He shut it, then walked around to my side, opening my door and extending a hand to help me get out.

It was dark except for the glow of my porch light and the reflection off the snow. The air was cold and crisp, eerily still as snowy nights often are. I smelled the warm odor of a neighbor's woodstove and the faint aroma of evergreens. Balancing myself with the help of Judge Beck, I waited for him to shut and lock the SUV, then walked by his side, my arm tight in the grip of his hand, as we made our way to the front door.

That's when I saw the ghost hovering at the top of my porch steps. For a brief second my heart raced thinking it was Eli, then I realized this was the ghost from tonight. Judge Reynolds' spirit. He hadn't been in the car with us. How the heck had he known where I lived? Did ghosts have some sort of tracking device when it came to me? Either way, he was there and I had a feeling he was coming in.

I tried not to shiver I walked through the cold aura that surrounded the spirit. The judge opened the front door, and sure enough the spirit entered behind us, hovering off to the side while the judge locked up. Taco came dashing out of the kitchen toward us, skidding to a stop and staring at the ghost. His back arched and he let out a low warning sound somewhere between a growl and a meow.

Good cat. Hopefully between the two of us we could manage to keep the ghost confined to the downstairs, out of my bedroom and bathroom. That was probably the best I could hope for until his killer was brought to justice.

"What's up with Taco?" Judge Beck frowned down at the annoyed cat.

"He sees a ghost," I told him, knowing he'd never believe me.

The judge knelt down. "Nothing's there Taco. It's all good, boy."

The cat sent the ghost another glare, then headed over to the judge purring and head butting the man's outstretched hand.

I slipped my heels off and set them aside, then took off my coat and hung it up, noticing that the ghost moved respectfully aside as I opened the closet door.

"I'm guessing from the way you were sleeping in the car that a nightcap is out of the question?"

I hesitated. Seeing him there in his tux with a purring cat in his arms made me want to stay, but I was exhausted and I knew that daylight would come early and Daisy would be here with the sunrise for yoga.

"Rain check? I'm so tired that you'd definitely need to carry me upstairs if I indulged. And from what you said in the car, I don't think that would be a pleasant experience for either of us."

He laughed. "I had a wonderful time this evening, Kay. I'm so sorry for the way it ended, but I still enjoyed your company."

"I did too." I covered a yawn. "Thank you for inviting me, and thank you..." I almost thanked him for the dress, but caught myself, "for helping when I found Judge Reynolds. And thank you for driving so far out of your way to take Ruby home."

He smiled, and suddenly he reminded me of a thirteen-year-old boy who had just brought a date home from the movies and wasn't sure whether to kiss her or not.

"I was happy to be there for you, Kay."

He put Taco down and headed up the stairs behind me. Our bedrooms were on the second floor, but both of us climbed to the third floor, peeking in to make sure Madison and Henry were both sound asleep in their rooms. On the way back down, Judge Beck hesitated as I stepped off the landing on the second floor.

"Aren't you going to bed?" I asked.

"Yeah, I just... was, uh, wondering if I should run out and get donuts for everyone tomorrow."

I'd been too busy to bake today, and the few lemon zest muffins I had left in the bread box wouldn't be enough for everyone. "That would be great. Or I could make pancakes."

He shook his head. "You're always feeding us, Kay. Let me at least provide some boxed donuts for you. What's your favorite? Apple spice? Sour cream?"

He was about to get the surprise of his life. "Glazed with chocolate frosting, or crullers with chocolate frosting if they have them."

"Got it." He grinned then turned toward his bedroom. "Sweet dreams, Kay."

"You too," I called out. Before he went into his room I thought I heard him muttering something but couldn't quite make out what it was.

I somehow managed to get my gown off on my own, laying it across a chair so I could take it to the dry cleaners this week. After putting on my pajamas, I padded down the hall to the bathroom to wash the make-up off and brush my teeth. Taco still hadn't come upstairs, so I headed back down and found my cat doing his best German Shepherd routine, guarding the ghost that he'd cornered by the hallway closet.

"Down boy." Obviously Taco did not respond to that command, so I gathered him into my arms and motioned for the ghost to follow me as I went into the kitchen.

Unlike most of the ghosts I'd encountered since my weird paranormal sensitivity had kicked in this year, Rhett Reynolds was polite and respectful...and obedient to my requests. From what I'd seen of him and from what his daughter had told me, I wasn't surprised.

I gave Taco a little bit of Happy Cat kibble in his bowl to distract him and sat on one of the island barstools facing the ghost.

"So, here's the deal. Yes, I discovered your body, but I'm not the one in charge of this investigation. You were a judge; you must know this. I'm nosy, so I'll definitely dig around, and anything I find out I'll turn over to the police, but I've got other things I need to do. I've got a job. And Christmas is coming up. I suggest you go haunt the detective in charge of your murder instead of hanging around me and my house."

My kitchen window frosted over and with a squeaking noise that made my ears hurt, a picture appeared.

An eye.

"I get it. I can see you, and the detective can't. But if you can draw a picture on a frosted window for me, you can do the same thing for him. Go guide him in the investigation."

The eye picture frosted over and was replaced by one word—Ruby.

It was like someone had my heart in a vise. "We made sure she got home safely. It's going to be very hard for her to get past your death, but she will eventually. She loves you. She hopes that she makes you proud."

I felt a wave of sorrow and regret, then an underline appeared in addition to the word on the window.

"I asked her to call me tomorrow and let me know how she was doing. I don't know what you want from me. I just met your daughter tonight. I'd be happy to be her friend, to make sure she gets through this, but that's her decision, not mine. I can't foist myself, a stranger, upon a grieving woman I just met. If you're concerned about her, maybe you should go visit one of her friends. Or her dog, Dolly."

The message on the frosty window went back to an eye.

"Look, I'm not the only person who can see you. In fact, I'm sure there are lots of mediums that can actually communicate with you in a method more effective than drawing in the frost on a window."

Again the window frosted and one word appeared on it. Trust.

I had no idea why Judge Reynolds' ghost would trust me. I'd just met him. I barely knew him. Maybe it was because I'd felt a surge of empathy toward his daughter and taken her under my wing. Maybe in death he'd developed the ability to see into my heart and soul and liked what he saw. Maybe he psychically knew there was some important role I'd play in this investigation, and he was trying to nudge me in the right direction.

For some reason, I thought it was the last one.

"Okay. No going in my bedroom or bathroom. Actually, please remain on this floor if you're inside the house. Please be respectful of private and family time, and conversations. I'll do what I can to help you and your daughter, but I can't promise anything. And I need you to agree that if your murder case isn't solved in the next month, you'll go somewhere else."

My final request was a long shot. I had no way of enforcing that beyond calling Olive and I wasn't even sure *she* could make that sort of banishment stick. I really didn't want to face the prospect that this ghost would be a permanent resident of my house. Sometimes murders went unsolved, and sometimes the wrong person was convicted of the crime. Me having to deal with a ghost in my home couldn't be a consequence of that, especially since the investigation was really out of my hands.

Agreed.

Clearly Rhett Reynolds was a good man in death as he was in life. It made me even more determined to stick my nose into this investigation, and to make sure I helped Ruby in any way that I could.

The ghost slipped through the walls into some other part of the house. I watched the frost fade from the window, and when Taco was done eating the last of his kibble, I picked him up and went upstairs to bed.

CHAPTER 7

I was bleary eyed but up with the dawn to do yoga with Daisy. She wanted to go out into the snow and do sun salutations, but I convinced her the basement would be better. My new ghost resident stayed out of our way. I'd seen him back by the hallway closet and near the back door, but he hadn't followed us down for yoga.

"I got J.T.'s present," Daisy announced as we began.

I eyed her from my upside-down position. "And?"

My friend grinned. "A GoPro. That way he can do some chase scenes for his YouTube channel. Action shots will really add to the videos."

I imagined a shaky video of J.T. running down a bail-jumper and bit back a smile. "He'll love it."

"What did you get the judge?" Daisy asked as she moved into a plank.

I had no idea what to get my roommate. "Nothing yet. Madison and I are going shopping this afternoon. Hopefully I'll get inspired."

"No ideas after your party?" She smirked over at me.

"The party where I found a murdered man in a bath-

85

room? The party that pretty much ended because the entire police force descended on us to interview all the attendees? The party after which the judge and I ended up driving the daughter of the murdered man home?"

"What? *What?*"

I know it was horrible of me to joke about a homicide, but I loved surprising Daisy like this. I told her about the party, my discovery in the upstairs restroom, and about the ghost now lurking about my house.

"I was expecting you to tell me about a slow dance, a kiss goodnight, and maybe more." Daisy laughed. "I should have known better. Only you can end up finding a murdered man in what was supposed to be a romantic evening out."

I followed her into a downward dog pose. "It wasn't really supposed to be a romantic evening, Daisy. Judge Beck wanted to attend as part of his career advancement and needed a plus-one."

Daisy snorted. "Yep, that's why he bought you an amazing dress and had his daughter hide it in the back of your closet."

"Shhh!" I glanced up the stairs. "He doesn't know that I know."

I was pretty sure Daisy was rolling her eyes, but since we were in a Uttanasana pose, I couldn't tell.

"Throw me a bone here, Carrera. There's got to be at least one romantic thing that happened last night."

She'd had made no secret of her desire to see the judge and I in love. It's not like I could deny my attraction or budding feelings. Daisy always saw right through that. Besides, she was my best friend, and I couldn't help but be honest with her even if I wasn't always honest with myself.

I glanced toward the stairs again. There had been foot-steps above earlier, but I was pretty sure I'd heard the door close. Either way, I decided to keep my voice as low as possible.

"We danced. It was a slow dance, and it was…" I pursed my lips, trying to find a way to describe it.

"Sexy? You guys were grinding all up against each other on the dance floor, right?"

I laughed. "To 'Rhapsody on a Theme of Paganini'? Hardly. It was magic. It was like a movie. It was electric."

"And then?" Daisy abandoned any pretense at yoga and stood.

"I had to go to the bathroom."

This time I did see her eyes roll. "You chickened out and ran off, afraid of the electricity. Am I right?"

How well she knew me. "Partially. I did have to go, and I needed a minute to process everything. Judge Beck went to get me another glass of wine. I think…well, I don't know what would have happened, but that's when I found the murder victim, and that kind of ruined the whole romantic mood."

"Not necessarily." Daisy sat down on the floor cross-legged. "Come on, Kay. I doubt even a dead body could extinguish those flames. Talk to me."

"When I found the dead man I didn't call 911, I called Judge Beck. He started ordering people around, glared his way past the security guards, and came running down the hall to me."

Daisy put her chin in her hands. "Go on."

"When we got home and we'd checked on the kids, he stopped at the second-floor landing, and I think he might have been going to kiss me. Maybe I'm wrong though. It was just kind of weird and awkward, and I didn't think about it until the moment had passed so it's not like I sent him any signals that I'd welcome that."

I'd expected Daisy to throw up her hands in exasperation and berate my lack of romantic instincts, but instead she grinned.

"That's okay. There will be another time."

Then she said something that completely surprised me.

"Take your time, Kay. You were married to Eli for a long time, and this has been a year of huge change for you. Judge Beck is a patient man. He's not in any hurry and neither should you be. When it feels right, let your feelings show, but don't ever think you need to rush."

I sank down on the carpet next to her. "Thank you. That makes me feel so much better. I've been beating myself up for even imagining any sort of relationship with Eli not even gone a year yet. Then I'm beating myself up for being a scared fool and running away from what might be awesome. Honestly I'm scared."

She chuckled. "Look at how long J.T. and I have been dating. I still get scared. I'm sure he still gets scared."

True. It had taken them forever to move their relationship to a physical level. The pair of them seemed very happy together moving things along at their own pace. The one thing I'd learned from watching my best friend and J.T. was that every relationship danced to its own music. What was right for them was right, no matter what the conventional formula for a successful relationship might be.

I definitely heard the door open and close that time. "Judge Beck is getting donuts this morning," I told Daisy.

"Donuts?" She got to her feet. "Yoga ends early today. I want a donut and some coffee."

She held out a hand and I let her help me up, because coffee and a chocolate-covered donut was exactly what I needed right now. Exactly.

* * *

I WAS on my way to the mall with Madison when my phone rang, announcing the caller to be Ruby. Thinking I needed to probably get some sort of Bluetooth device, I answered the phone and let Ruby know she was on speaker.

"I'm calling to check in and let you know I survived the night." She sounded better—less tired and stunned. The voice on the phone was the same dry, snarky Ruby I'd spoken to early last night, before her father's murder.

"I'm glad." I glanced over at Madison, carefully choosing my words. "Anything I can do to help?"

She sighed. "Well, I don't think I'll be wanting beer or wine any time soon. I don't know when they're releasing Dad's car, or when I'm free to make arrangements. I really don't feel up to going through his condo yet. Maybe I'll do that later this week."

"If you need someone around to help sort through clothing and kitchen utensils, let me know," I told her. "I've been there, and I know it can feel a bit overwhelming to do it all yourself."

"Thank you. My mother lives in Seattle and we aren't very close. I've got a few friends who can help, but I don't want to overwhelm them. And knowing how much stuff my dad has, it might be better to go through his stuff one day a week over a month or two."

I remembered my promise to the ghost of her father, but I barely knew Ruby. I'd suggest ways I could help, but it's not like I was in any position to just swing by her house and check on her, or pester her with offers of assistance. "Let me know what I can do. And please call me if you need anything."

Madison turned to me as I hung up. "A friend of yours? Did her father die?"

"He did. It was very unexpected."

The girl chewed on her lip. "Does she have any brothers or sisters? I heard her say she wasn't close to her mother."

"I don't think so. I haven't known her very long, but I've never heard her mention a sibling."

She was silent for a few minutes as I navigated through traffic toward the mall.

"I don't know what I'd do if Dad died," she said so softly I could barely hear her.

My breath lodged in my throat at the thought. "Oh, honey. Your father is healthy and young. You've got a long time with him before you have to face that."

"But what if I don't?" She chewed on her lip again. "You said your friend's father died unexpectedly. You told me about your husband's accident and how he almost died. What if that happens to Dad? What if he has a horrible car accident on the way to work one morning? What if he has a massive heart attack, or an aneurism, or flesh-eating bacteria or something?"

"I can't say those things never happen, but the chances of them occurring are pretty slim." I glanced over at her. "You have two parents who love you dearly. You've got a brother who you might think is a giant pain in the butt right now, but who will always be there when you need him, just as you'll be there for him. And, there's me. I love you and Henry, and I would do anything for the pair of you. Never forget that."

She smiled over at me. "I love you too, Kay."

It made me think of Ruby. Her mother across the country and not someone she could reach out to. No siblings. Her father murdered. And it was Christmas.

I needed to invite Ruby to join us. And I needed to change the topic of conversation. This was supposed to be a fun shopping trip for Madison and I. Fun. Not thinking of who might die and when.

"So what store should we go to first?" I asked her as I turned into the mall parking lot.

"Sephora." The glance Madison sent my way was downright impish.

"To buy your mother a gift or pick something up for yourself? Because I doubt you're buying Henry or your father a gift from a cosmetics store."

She laughed. "Okay, okay. But if we get all our shopping done before dinner, I want to check out some mascara."

I headed toward the center of the mall, realizing that if I had any hope of finding a parking space in the next half an hour, I'd need to just find something at the outer edges and walk in.

"So, as I asked before, where first?"

"Nordstrom."

I parked, even though I was as far from Nordstrom as possible while still in the mall parking lot. I couldn't remember the last time I'd been in that store. Honestly, I couldn't remember the last time I'd been in this mall. Two, three years ago? Maybe longer. No, two years ago when I'd been getting those shirts from Jos. A. Bank that Eli had loved.

I wondered if Judge Beck liked shirts from Jos. A. Bank.

I put the car in park, turned it off, and grabbed my purse. "Nordstrom it is. And on the way, maybe we'll grab a smoothie."

"Or a HoneyBaked ham." Madison grabbed her purse and jumped out of the car. "I'm ready to shop, Kay. How about you?"

I grinned at her enthusiasm. "Oh, I am *so* ready to shop, Madison. So ready."

CHAPTER 8

"*H*ow about this?" Madison made an Instagram-ready pouty face as she held up the bright pink North Face jacket.

I laughed. "Cute. Are you shopping for yourself again?"

"No, I'm shopping for Dad."

Right. "Have you ever seen your father wear a pink puffy jacket?"

She smirked. "Well, maybe he should."

That's how our shopping trip had been so far, and I wasn't exactly sad about it. Madison was charming, funny, and clever, and I was really enjoying her company. But in spite of that, we weren't getting much done in the way of our holiday shopping."

"Seriously, Madison? If you're going to spend two hundred dollars on something at least make it something your Dad is going to actually wear."

She fake-pouted once more. "Are you saying he wouldn't wear it?"

This girl had her father tightly wrapped around her pinky, and she knew it. "You know darned well that your dad would wear that thing just because you bought it for him, but why torture him so?"

She slid the jacket back onto the rack with a grin. "Okay, okay. This sort of thing worked when I was five. I don't think it would work now. He'd know it was a prank. And you're right—a pink puffy coat is probably pushing things a bit too far."

Madison liked to save all her gift-buying for the week before Christmas, so she had quite a list of gifts to buy between her family and her friends. I'd knitted most of my gifts, but I still needed to find something for Judge Beck.

It seemed half the county had the same idea because the mall was jam-packed with frazzled shoppers, blindly throwing random items in carts in an effort to just get it all over with and get back to the eggnog.

At least that's what I was thinking.

"How about we head over to the sporting goods store?" I suggested. "We can get your dad a new golf club or something."

"Nope." Madison waved her hand as if she were Oprah announcing a giveaway. "Everyone gets clothes. I'm upping the fashion-game for the men in my family, starting with Dad."

"Well then let's move away from the pink puffy coats." I wove around a family with a double stroller into a section with dressier coats. "How about this one?"

It was a three-quarter length black merino wool and cashmere coat. Masculine, elegant, soft. I could absolutely see Judge Beck wearing this sort of coat every day.

Madison scrunched up her face. "He has one exactly like that."

Which was probably why I could imagine Judge Beck wearing this sort of coat every day.

"He looks like a judge all the time," Madison complained. "Even when he's off work, he looks like a judge."

I felt slightly offended on her father's behalf. "He wore shorts and a polo shirt at the barbeque. And he wears khakis with a polo shirt when he plays golf."

The teen rolled her eyes. "That's judge-not-working clothes. He doesn't own *anything* hip."

"He wears cartoon-print pajamas and an old brewery t-shirt," I shot back. The judge alternated between plaid ones, ones with fishes on them, ones with little Hello Kittys, and the ones with Pokémon characters.

Although now that I thought about it, my comment sounded...intimate. Yes, the judge lived in my house, but the admission that I'd seen Madison's father wandering around in his pajamas was a bit embarrassing.

"Who do you think got him those pajamas?" Madison rolled her eyes again. "And those race and brewery shirts were from when he was young and cool. Mom kept trying to throw them away and dad always dug them out of the donation bag."

I loved the judge's quirky pajamas and ratty t-shirts. Maybe I needed to give Madison more credit and let her choose whatever she wanted for her father. It *was* her gift after all.

"Okay. You win. Let's make your father totally rad."

An hour later we were stuffing bags into the car. She'd gotten him jeans, more t-shirts, a distressed leather bomber jacket, and a North Face coat in a more suitable color than bright pink. I'd been a little shocked at the numbers ringing up on the cash register, but Madison had handed over a credit card with the sort of casual nonchalance of a girl who'd never wanted for anything.

It made me uncomfortable. At her age I'd been carefully spending babysitting money for my Christmas gifts, not charging it all on my father's credit card. I know times were different, that both she and Henry were good children and far from entitled brats, but I still wondered if they ever thought about how fortunate they really were.

We headed back inside and Madison got to work on Henry's clothing makeover. I browsed through the housewares section, feeling like I was in a Hallmark Christmas movie at the moment. I'd made scarves for my friends and for Madison. I'd bought Henry an out-of-print book of pre-Revolutionary furniture styles in the colonies. I'd was thinking of getting Judge Beck an electronic picture frame and loading it up with various pictures I'd snapped of us and the kids throughout the year. Now I was having a twinge of regret, wondering if that was enough. Here I was faced with all this excess, thinking that maybe I should be spending more on the people I cared about most in my life.

I had no luxurious long hair to sell like Della in return for a watch fob chain, and that story hadn't worked out so well in the end anyway. Gifts were supposed to come from the heart. I'd carefully chosen each of mine so that they held meaning both to me and hopefully to the recipient. What I'd spent, or not spent, on them was immaterial, so I paid for the electronic picture frame and decided to make it the best gift I could.

"Oh, Kay! Look!"

She was holding a cable-knitted hat with ears and whiskers along the brim. Before I could comment, Madison had crammed it onto my head.

"You look like Taco!" she announced.

I had a bad feeling this was going to be my gift. "It's so cute!" I exclaimed. "I love the ears. And it's really warm with the fleece inside."

Maybe I'd wear it sitting out back drinking coffee on cold January weekends. Or maybe I'd say "screw it" and wear it to work. Suddenly I thought of the pink North Face jacket and knew exactly how Judge Beck had felt all these years. I loved these kids, and I'd proudly wear anything they gave me, whether it was a macaroni necklace or a hat with cat ears and whiskers.

"I got one for Henry that looks like Cthulhu. Only red, so maybe it's supposed to be Doctor Zoidberg from Futurama."

She snatched the hat off my head and ran back to her overflowing cart. I found myself staring after her, a completely besotted smile on my face.

I loved these kids. I loved them so much. No matter where their future took them, no matter where my future took *me*, I'd always cherish these memories. And I'd wear that darned hat every single day if one of them bought it for me.

After shopping, Madison and I went to dinner together. We sat together over burgers and fries, planning out Christmas dinner and deciding which of us would cook what foods.

"I saw what happened at the party last night," she announced, out of the blue in typical teenager fashion. "About Judge Reynolds being killed."

I sat down my burger. "Where did you hear that?" There had been a brief mention on the radio about Judge Reynolds dying, but no details, let alone that foul play was suspected.

"Twitter. It's where you find everything out, like super-fast. I read a tweet just now that said he was beaten to death in a bathroom during the party. I'm glad I didn't know before I went to bed, or I would have been frantically texting Dad all night. He never tells us stuff like that. Should I be worried? A judge was murdered. Dad's a judge. Kay, is he in danger?"

"He's not," I reassured him. "This had nothing to do with him, or with his job. The police will find out who did this, but I'm sure it was someone from Judge Reynolds' past or personal life."

She picked at a few of her fries. "I wonder if Mom knows. She used to go to all those parties with Dad, and socialized with all the wives. When Dad became a judge, Mom made a list of the other judges and their families. She'd invite them to the country club, or to lunch, or coffee. She probably knows him, I guess."

"If she knows Judge Reynolds, then I'm sure knows of his death by now," I told the girl. Thinking I might want to mention it to Heather when she came to pick up the kids tonight. It worried me that this was the second conversation I was having with Madison where she was concerned about her father dying. It was something both her parents should know about.

I suddenly thought of something else. "Did you get your mom a gift yet? And her boyfriend..." Drat, I'd forgotten his name.

"Tyler." She nodded. "I got them both gifts."

There was something in the extremely unenthusiastic way she said that which made me think she hadn't enjoyed buying one or both of those gifts. It wasn't my business to pry about her mother or her mother's boyfriend, but I'd heard Daisy talk too often about the kids she worked with not to at least encourage Madison to share anything she wanted with me.

"Everything okay?" I asked. "With your mom? With Tyler?" I'm sure Daisy would have worded it better, but it was the best I could do.

Madison nodded. "I guess. He's okay. Kinda boring, if you ask me."

"Weren't you just saying your father was boring?" I teased.

She laughed at that. "Dad *dresses* boring, but he's not

97

boring. Tyler is. He's nice to mom. He's nice to Henry and me. He took us all on that cruise this summer. That was fun."

"But?" I pressed.

She sighed. "He works for some company managing people or something. He goes to work at eight, is home at five-thirty on the dot. Never brings work home with him, never works on weekends."

"That sounds nice." I tried to word this as carefully as possible. "It sounds like what your mom wanted."

"It's what Mom thought she wanted," Madison blurted out. "He's nice, he's reliable and dependable, and he seems to love her. But there's no interesting talk about cases, or law, or politics, or current events."

"What *you* want in a romantic partner might not be what your mother wants," I told her. "As long as he treats her, and both you and your brother, right and she's happy—those are the important things."

She fidgeted with the straw in her soda. "I want someone who loves his job—who sees it as a career, as his passion. I want us both to come home and be excited to talk about what we've done and how it impacts the world, or our society, or something. I want to do something that matters, and I want my boyfriend, or husband, to do something that matters."

Like a surgeon or a judge, or a journalist turned skip tracer and junior investigator.

"The world needs plumbers, car salespeople, and sanitation workers too," I reminded her. "And the world needs people working for corporations who manage other people. Those things might not sound exciting to you, but they *are* important. And to many people, a job is what pays the bills so they can spend their free time doing what they're passionate about."

She sighed. "I know, I know. I wouldn't mind so much if

Tyler spent his free time helping the homeless, or doing something artistic."

"What does Tyler do in his free time?"

She thought for a second. "Watches a lot of TV. He golfs."

I didn't point out that her father golfed, and that both she and Henry enjoyed spending hours in front of the television. Of course, Tyler was probably watching different sorts of shows than Madison and Henry did.

"What did you get him for Christmas?" I asked, curious.

She made a face. "A pen set for his office. I had no idea what to get him. They're nice pens."

"And your mom?"

"Monthly mani-pedis for a year." Madison shoved a fry into her mouth. "She used to go every month when she and Dad were together, but I noticed she hasn't been going anymore."

I felt a bit sad about that, but it seemed everyone needed to make lifestyle changes during a divorce. Judge Beck was renting rooms in my house. Heather had to give up some of her luxuries.

It made me wonder what Helen Dixon had to give up leaving her husband for Judge Reynolds. She'd been at the party last night. Was she invited on her own, or was she the guest of someone else? Had she and her husband gotten back together after the relationship with Rhett Reynolds hadn't worked out?

I put the thoughts aside and concentrated on my food. After a few moments of silence, Madison suddenly snorted out a laugh.

"You know, I'll bet plumbers have good stories to tell when they get home from work."

I grinned. "Like about what they found crammed down someone's clogged toilet?"

"Or in the washing machine drain?"

"Two feet of water in someone's basement from a water main break?"

"Overflowing tub that crashed through the ceiling into the living room?"

By now we were both nearly crying with laughter. "Maybe you should become a plumber," I told Madison. "You'd definitely be making a difference in people's lives. When people need a plumber, they usually *really* need a plumber."

"Ewww. Yuck." She wrinkled her nose. "All that septic system stuff. And toilets. Have you seen how messy guys are when they pee? I'm not crawling around the base of a toilet for a living. No way. And plumbers don't wear cool clothes either."

We made it home before the judge and Henry. Madison dashed up the stairs to wrap her gifts while I stashed what I'd bought in my bedroom and went downstairs to decide what to have for dinner. I was just about to pull some ground beef out of the freezer when I heard a knock on the door.

Heather stood outside, shifting her weight nervously from foot to foot. "Hi Kay. I'm here early and thought it would be weird and kind of creepy if I just sat in my car. Can I come in?"

"Of course!" I opened the door wider. "Madison is upstairs, but she's wrapping gifts and doesn't want anyone to see. Come join me in the kitchen,"

I led her through the house, telling her to go ahead and sit on one of the stools. "Can I get you some coffee? Hot tea? Iced tea?" I asked holding up the kettle.

"Oh, I really don't want to be a bother."

As if pouring something in a glass or mug was a bother.

"Well If you want hot tea, that's what I'm making for myself." I pulled two cups out of the cabinet and sat one in front of her. "The box of teas is right there. Go ahead and pick out what you'd like."

Heather made herself busy with the teas while I put the kettle on and began defrosting the ground beef. Finally she selected a ginger peach herbal tea.

"Good choice," I told her. "Are you done your shopping yet?"

"Pretty much. I've got stocking stuffers to get, but I like to grab those at the last minute."

I had some decorative stockings I'd hung from the mantel, but hadn't thought about filling them at Madison's and Henry's age. Heather must have seen my surprised expression because she laughed.

"I know, I know. It's just me being sentimental. I've never been able to give up playing Santa, although the past few years the stockings mostly have hair ties, nail clippers, and USB sticks among the candy. They'll be grown and gone and I'll still be filling their stockings."

"That's a nice tradition."

We chatted about our childhood Christmases while I started browning the ground beef. When the kettle whistled, I filled the pot and put the tea in to steep.

"Did you hear about what happened with Judge Reynolds last night?" I asked as I took the stool opposite Heather.

She nodded. "I heard it on the news this morning and couldn't believe it. I've been to those parties with Nate a few times and security is always tight."

"They had guards everywhere last night." Oops. Did she know I'd gone with her soon-to-be ex-husband? Deciding I better explain further, I continued. "He wanted to attend and asked if I'd accompany him. It was a great opportunity to network and hopefully bring in more clients."

She slowly shook her head, not appearing at all bothered that I'd gone to the party with Judge Beck. "I really didn't know Rhett Reynolds that well. He pretty much stayed in his county. He wasn't one to go to all the social functions. I was really shocked when I heard he and Judge Dixon's wife had been having an affair. How the heck did he meet her? Helen isn't the sort of woman to be hanging out in Polefax County, and he is absolutely not her type at all. I mean, he's not exactly an Adonis nor is he rich and powerful."

"And then he dumps her," I said, pouring our tea and nudging the sugar over to Heather.

"At least Helen made out like a bandit in the divorce." Heather scooped a spoonful of sugar into her cup and stirred it. "I was convinced Stuart Dixon would find a way to make sure Helen walked with only the clothes on her back, but the woman is set for life. Fastest divorce ever. Belinda said it took their lawyers all of five minutes to type it up and it was done. They'd agreed on everything beforehand. Weird."

"Do you think she killed him? Or his ex-wife?"

Heather looked up in surprise from her tea. "Helen? Are you kidding? I'm willing to bet she had a new man on her arm five minutes after Rhett broke it off—*if* he was really the one who broke it off."

"Really?" I frowned, trying to remember who had said Rhett Reynolds had broken the relationship off, and that Helen was upset over it. Maybe they were wrong. Maybe they didn't know Helen Dixon as well as Heather seemed to have.

"You know…" Heather sipped her tea pensively. "I'd be willing to bet that Helen used Rhett as a way to get a divorce from Stuart. He's never cared about her affairs with the tennis instructor or the guy behind the counter at the coffee shop, but he'd never turn a blind eye to Helen having an affair with one of his peers."

"But if she wanted a divorce, why not just tell him and start the proceedings herself? It's not like the man has to do that. I can't see any advantage to taking up with Judge Reynolds to make her husband divorce her." A horrible thought went through my mind. "Unless he was one of those controlling jerks who never would have consented to a divorce otherwise."

But that didn't make sense either. If Stuart Dixon was one of those sort of men, then he hardly would have quickly and easily divorced the woman who'd cheated on him with a peer —or agreed to let her have more than half of the marital property.

Heather shrugged. "The fire had gone out between him and Helen a decade ago. At this point, theirs was more a marriage of finances and gracing the society pages. Stuart was probably relieved. Although I still can't believe he let her walk with so much money. There might not have been any passion left between them, but he loves his money just as much as Helen does."

Helen Dixon moved down a few notches on my suspect list, but I wasn't ready to let her go yet. I still wanted to hear a few more opinions about the woman's affair with Rhett Reynolds to completely cross her off. Her ex-husband, though, was moving into one of my top spots. Heather might not think he cared enough about Helen to kill out of jealousy, but there was still the money. Rhett Reynolds had caused his divorce and cost him a lot of money in the proceedings. But if he was angry enough about that to kill Rhett Reynolds, then would Helen be the next to die? Although the murder of both his ex-wife *and* her lover would put the police right at his door. So perhaps Helen was safe for now.

"Mom!" Madison bustled into the kitchen and gave her mother a hug. "You're early."

Heather lifted her cup. "Just having some tea with Miss Kay and talking over Christmas traditions."

Madison glanced over my way. "Miss Kay, do you mind if Mom and I go into the front room?"

Ah Christmas. It was a time for secrets.

"Go right ahead. Heather, fill up your teacup first. I'll stay in here and work on dinner."

Which I'd decided was going to be stuffed cabbage. I had no idea if the judge would want any or not, but stuffed cabbage was a comfort food I'd grown up with. Just the idea brought back memories of childhood winters, my mom at the stove while I read or colored at a little child-sized table in the corner.

Heather and Madison left, and in their place a ghost appeared.

"Thank you. I appreciate you not hovering around while I had a guest."

I could have sworn the ghost nodded. Again my kitchen window frosted over and the word "Ruby" appeared.

"She called me when Madison and I were on the way to the mall," I told the ghost. "She's doing better this morning. I offered to help her go through your things when she's ready. If I don't hear from her in a few days, I'll call and invite her to lunch or something."

Two lines appeared under the word on the window. What did he mean? I'm sure he was worried about his daughter. It was clear they'd been close, and I could believe he'd still be concerned about her after his death, but what exactly did he want me to do?

"Can't you go visit her yourself? I know she can't see you, but you could communicate with her like this—with words written on the window. And that way you'd be able to see firsthand how she's doing."

The frost suddenly melted off the window, leaving me unenlightened. Maybe the spirit could only do this around me? Maybe something kept him from going to see his daughter, that tied him to me and my house? I eyed the window and had one of those "duh" moments.

"Who killed you, Rhett? Write the name on the window. Who killed you?"

The window frosted over and I held my breath. I could hardly go to the police and tell them a ghost revealed the name of his murderer, but if it would be a whole lot easier to look for proof if I knew who'd done it.

But a name didn't appear in the frost on the window. Instead there was a symbol—a dollar sign.

CHAPTER 9

*M*oney. Was that the motive? Had my wild idea about Stuart Dixon been right, or was there someone else at that party who had a financial motive to murder Rhett Reynolds? Those were the thoughts running through my mind all evening and during my morning yoga with Daisy.

Judge Beck had eaten the stuffed cabbage, even forcing out some compliments. Clearly that was going to have to be a dish I made when he was working late.

I pulled into the parking lot, easing my ancient sedan into a spot between J.T.'s Jeep and Molly's new Scion. "New" was a relative term. It was new to her after having been through several previous owners. It was a 2003, but it ran and in spite of its age wasn't rusting away into oblivion like mine was.

Molly Warner had been hired at my recommendation after she'd helped nab a killer, and I was thrilled to have her in the office. She was a quick learner, enthusiastic, and it meant I was no longer drowning in work. I hoped to eventually turn most of the routine skip tracing over to her in the next month and start to take on more cases with an actual investigative component.

"What, no muffins or scones?" J.T. lamented as he saw me walk into the office empty-handed.

"I had a busy weekend. I promise to do better."

"You better." Molly waved a finger at me. "I'm pretty sure home-baked goods are in my employment contract."

I held up my hands, conceding defeat. "Lemon zucchini bread tomorrow morning, I promise."

Now that I wasn't working three to four hours every night after work, I might be able to step up my cooking game a bit, although if I was being tasked with providing regular breakfast goods, J.T. was going to need to do their share as well.

"If you guys are going to demand baked goods, then I'm demanding lunches. Any time we have to work through lunch, the company pays."

J.T. winced. "Okay. But if this starts happening more than twice a week, I'll need to reconsider."

Cheap penny-pincher. I hoped he wasn't bargain hunting on Daisy's Christmas gift. Although from what I'd seen, J.T.'s frugal nature vanished whenever he was spending money on Daisy.

We spent a few hours going over our caseload, including a new batch of skip trace work from Creditcorp. It seems quite a few people had fallen on hard times during the holiday season, and we were supposed to dig up any information on current employment and residence. J.T. had four auto repossessions and two bail jumps, and four bail bond requests that needed processing.

All this made me feel bad about my job, as if I were a horrible person for tracking down people and ruining their holiday season. I know that they'd all made commitments on either appearing in court or paying their debts, and that they'd gone back on those commitments, but I still felt bad. Things happened. They'd happened to me. It could have been me J.T. was tracking down after Eli had died and I'd found myself overwhelmed in debt. I was still digging my way out of that hole. The judge's rent payments had been a help. My job and promotion had been a huge help. Month my month, dollar by dollar, I chipped away at the debt and hoped that in a year or two I'd be able to replace my car, replace appliances, and repair my home without falling to the edge of poverty.

Just before lunchtime I got a call that made me realize my dreams of a relaxing evening were going up in flames.

"The police want to talk to me," I told J.T. "It's about a murder victim I discovered at that swanky party I was at Saturday night."

Molly's eyes widened, her mouth forming a huge "O". J.T. laughed.

"I swear on all that's holy, Carrera. You can't even go to a holiday party without stumbling over a murder victim. Couldn't you just eat shrimp and avocado toast, and drink wine?"

"I tried, but all that wine meant I needed to use the restroom, and there was a murdered judge on the floor."

Molly let loose a few obscenities, a habit I was trying to cure her of. "Ooo, sorry! I mean, holy cow, Kay. A judge was murdered at a Christmas party? That's scary."

It had been scary, but a few days had put a few layers of protection and normalcy around the incident.

"Anyway, the police wanted to ask me a few questions, so I need to drive to the capital. Hopefully they won't keep me all day."

"You're not a suspect are you?" Molly practically danced with excitement over the prospect.

"I found the body. I was wearing a white dress that didn't

have one drop of blood splatter on it. And I was dancing with Judge Beck when the murder was likely to have occurred."

"They're hardly going to think a sixty-year-old woman in an evening gown is going to kill a man she just met." J.T. shot me a sideways glance. "Unless he took the last shrimp puff."

"I definitely could kill someone under the right circumstances, but it wouldn't be over a shrimp puff." I tossed an eraser at my boss. "I'll call you when I'm on my way back."

"I'll keep working on these skip traces and let you know where I am," Molly told me.

"And Kay?" J.T. tossed the eraser back at me. "This trip doesn't get expensed. It's not for a paying client."

Figures. Cheap penny-pincher of a boss.

* * *

OFFICER PERKINS WASN'T at this interview. Instead there was a woman with steel-gray hair in a severe shoulder-length cut with Bettie Page bangs. She introduced herself as Detective Burgess, and after procuring me a soda she sat opposite me.

Detective Burgess paged through a file for a few minutes before speaking up.

"So at the party, you spoke with Irene O'Donnell?"

"I spoke with a lot of people at the party, including Irene O'Donnell." I took a breath and counted the names off on my fingers. "One-on-one, I spoke with Horace Barnes and Justine Sanchez, the wife of Judge Sanchez. I spoke with Ruby Reynolds, the daughter of the deceased. I also spoke with Irene O'Donnell and the lieutenant governor."

"So tell me about your conversation with Irene O'Donnell."

I took a deep breath, knowing that I wasn't about to lie to the police. "She was really drunk," I began. "We went over to the bar and she ordered two wines. Then she asked me about my job as a private investigator and offered to hire me."

"And did she hire you?"

"Not as of this time. I didn't think I could help her, and told her so."

Bettie Page-Burgess fixed me with a thin-lipped glare. "What did she want your help with?"

"She'd been having some conflicts with Judge Reynolds in the courtroom and wanted me to check into his background."

"Did she seem upset? Angry?" The detective narrowed her eyes.

"She seemed drunk," I shot back. "I left her at the bar downing wine, and didn't see her after that."

The detective sat back in her chair. "You didn't see her at all the rest of the evening?"

I saw where she was going with this. "I'm guessing close to a hundred people were crowded into that party. There were a lot of people I never saw that evening, or only saw once."

She nodded and wrote a few things in her notepad.

"You know there are a lot of other people with a motive to kill Judge Reynolds," I volunteered. "The woman he dumped, Helen Dixon. Her husband that she cuckolded with Rhett Reynolds, Stuart Dixon. I'm sure there were even more people who might have wanted Judge Reynolds dead."

I didn't think a woman could have a more bored and disinterested expression on her face. "What exactly did Irene O'Donnell want you to dig up on Judge Reynolds?"

I waved a hand. "Nothing specific. Just anything that could possibly be enough of a scandal to get him unseated. She didn't murder him. She was drunk and it's a long stretch to go from wanting to find dirt in someone's background to bludgeoning them to death with a toilet tank lid."

Detective Burgess leaned forward onto the table. "How did you know it was a toilet tank lid? Cause of death and weapon has never been released to the press."

"I was there, remember?" I shot back. "I *saw* him. And I couldn't see anything in that restroom that might have been used to bludgeon someone. Those toilet tank lids are heavy. And in a restroom, they're conveniently at hand. Besides, it couldn't have been Irene. Blood splatter would have shown on Irene's dress." I suddenly thought of something. "You know who was wearing a red dress? Helen Dixon. Blood splatter wouldn't have shown on *her* dress."

I was pretty sure it would have, given that anything stains silk. Plus I couldn't see Helen Dixon bludgeoning someone to death either given what I'd been told about her. At this point I was just throwing things out there.

The detective fixed me with a long stare, then glanced back down at her notes. "Did you see anyone on the way upstairs? Someone standing near the elevator? In the hallway?"

I thought for a moment. "There were two security guards standing near the stairs. Lots of people dancing. No one was over by the elevator, or upstairs that I saw or even heard."

"What floor was the elevator on when you hit the call button?"

I frowned, closing my eyes to try to envision the scene. "Third, I think. I'm not positive."

The detective leaned back, a satisfied expression on her face. "One more question—do you remember seeing anyone in particular on the dance floor?"

Slowly I shook my head. "No, just a lot of men and women. About half the men had their jackets off, but that's really all I noticed. I was more concerned with getting to the elevator and the restroom at that point."

Detective Burgess scribbled a bit more in her notepad,

then stood. "Thank you for coming down, Mrs. Carrera. We'll let you know if we have any more questions."

I followed her out of the room and to the entrance of the station, then walked through the parking lot to my car. I was no closer to solving the mystery of who killed Judge Reynolds than when I'd come in. And I got the impression the police weren't any closer either.

CHAPTER 10

"*I*s this Kay Carrera with Pierson Investigations?" A woman asked, her voice vaguely familiar.

"Yes, it is. How can I help you?"

I had the phone on speaker, but pulled over to the side of the road when I realized this was a work call. I didn't have a work cell phone and had taken to giving my personal number out to any of my clients. I was guessing that J.T. must have given the woman my number. He hadn't told me of any new cases this morning though. It was a bit irritating that he was giving clients my number without briefing me first. Actually it was irritating that he wasn't paying my cell phone bill or providing me with one for work. That was definitely a conversation we needed to have sometime soon.

"This is Irene O'Donnell. I don't know if you remember me or not, but I met you last night at the holiday party?"

I would have been a horrible investigator if I hadn't remembered the woman who tried to hire me to dig up dirt on a judge even if I hadn't spent the last hour being grilled about that conversation by a police detective.

"Yes, I remember you." I looked around, feeling as if I

were in a forties film noir and wondering if there were plain-clothes detectives nearby, waiting for me to lead them to their suspect.

"I think...I think they're going to arrest me for Judge Reynolds' murder." Her voice raised in octave.

From the interview I'd just had at the very least they were going to question her, but I doubted the police were at the arrest stage of their investigation.

"You're not the only one with a broad motive, Irene," I said. "Just because Judge Reynolds ruled against some of your cases doesn't make you a top suspect for murder."

"It was a lot of cases. I've complained about him before, even made comments about how it would be a shame if he got run over by a bus or fell off a tall building. Everyone knew I had issues with the guy."

"And I'm sure others had issues as well." I tried to think through what I knew about the victim. "There was that affair he was having Helen Dixon. And he was known for contro-versial opinions, speaking his mind, and ruffling feathers. Irene, you're probably down near the bottom of a very long list of people who made their dislike of Judge Reynolds publicly known."

"I was at the party. And I'm sure my fingerprints are all over that bathroom."

"Because you work there?" Why had she called me? I'd just met her last night, and hadn't seen her at all after her drunken offer to hire me.

"I work on the third floor. Why would my fingerprints be in a second-floor restroom?"

"Because you were meeting another lawyer in his or her office, or in a conference room, or on your way up from the lobby and suddenly had to pee badly? Irene, none of this makes you a murder suspect."

It didn't, but I remembered how intent the detective had

been in her questioning and wondered if there was something she knew that I didn't, if there was something more than the circumstantial stuff Irene was telling me.

"I don't have an alibi," she blurted out. "I drank too much and didn't want anyone to see me puking my guts out in the bathroom, so I headed up to the third floor where my office is. I was at the party. I was gone the whole window of Judge Reynolds' murder. I've got no alibi, I've got motive, and my prints are in the restroom."

I thought back to the conversations I'd had with Judge Beck, the boring law books I'd been reading at night, my experience both as a journalist and a generally nosy person. This was all certainly enough to put a spotlight on Irene, but no jury would convict based on this alone. It all could be explained away by a good lawyer. Which was what Irene needed if she truly felt she was about to be arrested.

"If they want to talk to you again, have your lawyer present," I warned. "And don't represent yourself. Get someone else to look after your interests."

Irene snorted. "I'm not such an idiot as to represent myself in a possible murder case. I've got a lawyer, but I want to hire you. I know you refused before, but this time it's not just about my career. I need you to dig up everything you can so that if they charge me, my lawyer can show that one, or a dozen, people have the same means, motive, and opportunity as me to do Judge Reynolds in."

Ah. So that was the reason J.T. had given her my number. Yes, she'd probably asked for me, but any client I brought on myself was mine through our agreement. And I'd get a finder's fee as well.

I went over my rates, well aware that Irene probably knew all about the fees and incidental expenses involved in hiring an investigative service. Then I took down her e-mail address, letting her know that I'd forward her a contract and would begin as soon as I received the signed copy back.

"Consider it done," she replied.

I climbed into my car to head back to the office so I could send over the contract and go ahead and get started, because I had a new client. And the case I'd been interested in as a curious onlooker had suddenly become work.

J.T. and Molly were both out of the office when I got back, so I got right to work on my newest client. Irene sent the contract right back along with her credit card number for the retainer fee and the name and number of the attorney that would be representing her if what she feared happened and she got arrested or called in for additional questioning.

I eyed the background checks and skip traces on my desk realizing it might be another evening where I was working from my dining room table. Molly had enough to do on her own, and some of these were a bit more involved than she was ready to handle. I sorted through them, gathering up the ones with a deadline of tomorrow and putting them in my briefcase. Then I got to work on the more interesting case.

Figuring I needed to know as much as I could about the victim, I started with Judge Reynolds, adding his ex-wife as well as his daughter Ruby to the search. The only documents on my public case search that included Rhett Reynolds were about his divorce, which seemed to have been fairly quick and painless, and child support for Ruby.

Ruby was squeaky clean aside from a speeding ticket four years ago. I had to pull the former Mrs. Reynolds' name from the divorce record and search for both Elizabeth Reynolds and Elizabeth Crum in our state as well as Washington. Her record in both states was equally bland, but online case search only went back so far and both Elizabeth and Rhett were my age. That meant there was a good bit of their life on microfiche and not on my handy-dandy case search databases.

But where the courts mostly didn't bother to scan and add old cases to the database, newspapers tended to do so. Many of them only pulled up a teaser sentence or two on a search with the rest behind a paid archive firewall. I had a retainer and a nice allotment for expenses, so I went ahead and dug around, finding out where Ruby and her father went to college, where they both had worked and lived. Elizabeth seemed unlikely to be involved in this case, so I put her search to the side and concentrated on the two Reynoldses who hadn't been living in Seattle for the last ten years.

By the time I got ready to leave the office, I'd discovered that Rhett Reynolds had been outspoken about human rights issues, ethics, conflicts of interest in politicians, and campaign finance reform. He'd published op-ed pieces quite a bit in local papers as well as his college journal. He entered law school just as Ronald Reagan was entering the White House and was a progressive liberal at a time when the country was tilting toward the right. None of that seemed to hurt his prospects and he'd landed with a prominent firm right out of law school.

From there, I found chamber of commerce articles on his public service right alongside newspaper articles about his high-profile cases. He was the people's lawyer, taking on clients that no one else would take, often on a pro-bono basis. He went on the record scolding politicians for what he considered to be a dereliction of fiduciary responsibility, and became known as the no-nonsense, straight-talk guy who looked out for the little guy.

It seemed he was destined to a career as a litigation attorney taking class action lawsuits and appearing on television ads telling viewers he'd fight for their rights, but instead an opening occurred at the Polefax County Court. The citizens staged a massive write-in campaign and petitions demanding Rhett Reynolds be appointed, and it being an election year and all, the governor acquiesced.

Ruby had grown up in her father's shadow and seemed happy to follow in his footsteps from what I could see of her academic and job history. But where Rhett had a cult-of-personality thing going, Ruby worked more behind the scenes, tackling cases with the ferocity of a dog with a bone. She'd left the post-graduate big law firm after a few years, joining a smaller firm that was affiliated with several non-profits and focused on civil liberty and human rights cases. Just before I left the office, I pulled her credit report and saw that she managed to live on a modest salary, keeping her expenses well within her means.

I drove home, mulling it all over as Dire Straits sang "Sultans of Swing" on my radio. A person like Judge Rhett Reynolds would have bruised a lot of egos, probably made quite a few enemies before he'd even walked into his judge's chambers. But I couldn't see how the killer would have been anyone outside of that party. With all the judges, half a dozen city councilmen and women, and the lieutenant governor, the security had been tight.

Well, except for that elevator upstairs.

There had been nearly a hundred people at that party. Figuring out who might have had motive to kill Rhett Reynolds would be a herculean task if I looked at the entirety of his career. This had to be something recent—within the last few years recent. And it had to have been something that was escalating in the recent month or two. Searching the background of Judge Reynolds and his family would give me a good foundation for my investigation, but it wouldn't lead me directly to the killer. No, to do that I'd need a list of the party attendees as well as the cases the judge had ruled on in the last few years.

Plus there were a few other avenues to explore. One was Rhett's relationship with Judge Dixon's wife. The other was his nomination to the appellate court opening. Yes, everyone including his own daughter had said he wasn't likely to get the position, but something made me think the nomination might have been a factor. Maybe it had been a last straw, one final affront that made the killer snap and bludgeon Judge Reynolds to death in that upstairs bathroom.

It was a bit sad coming home to an empty house after a week of Judge Beck and the kids arriving right after school or sports practice. Still, Taco welcomed me, meowing loudly and jumping up to grab my leg with soft paws. I picked him up and he rubbed his face against mine, as he purred loudly.

"Yes, yes. I know you're hungry." I laughed and let him outside, knowing he'd be around at the back door in half an hour demanding his dinner.

Unpacking my briefcase on the dining room table, I went into the kitchen and started a pot of coffee, sorting through the mail before pouring some kibble into Taco's bowl. It was shaping up to be a long night of work, and Judge Beck's absence hinted that he'd be facing the same whenever he walked through the door. I rummaged through the fridge, slicing some cheese and putting it on the dining room table along with a box of crackers. That was going to be the extent of my cooking skills tonight.

Letting Taco in, I poured myself a cup of coffee and while the cat ate, I headed into the dining room. I really needed to get to work on the background checks and skip traces, but the attendee list from the party was sitting in my e-mail box courtesy of Irene's attorney, and I couldn't help but keep working on the case.

As I pored over the articles, my notes, and the list, a few things stood out as significant as it pertained to SMS&C. Stuart Dixon had worked for them twenty years ago and had been the lead attorney on the Cresswell class action suit. He'd been married to Helen for three years at that point and her brother had been an attorney there when the two had met. Sonny Magoo had also worked at SMS&C nearly thirty years ago, although the firm had been SM&S at that time. Announcements in the business section of the paper showed that he'd left them for another large firm across town and had been his firm's lead attorney on the Cresswell settlement for their clients.

Another name that frequently came up was Horace Barnes. Even though he never worked at the same firms as Magoo and Dixon, he did seem to be involved in several of their cases, and was pictured in the company of both men at several business functions from articles in the paper over the last thirty years.

I made a note to go visit Horace Barnes tomorrow, hoping he could shine a light on all this. Then I looked over to the corner of the dining room where the ghost of Rhett Reynolds stood quietly.

"Who killed you?" I asked again. The dining room window frosted over, but once more the ghost only drew a dollar sign.

Clearly the ghost was going to be of no further help, and my eyes were beginning to blur from the sheer volume of information I was trying to sift through. Reluctantly, I put the Reynolds murder aside and started in on the background checks and skip traces that I absolutely had to complete before I went to bed tonight.

I'd just finished and had turned back to the murder case when Judge Beck came in and plopped a box of folders on the table.

"Wasn't sure you'd still be up."

I held up a notepad full of scribbles, arrows, and sideways

notes. "I've been hired to do some work on the Reynolds murder."

His eyebrows shot up. "By his daughter? I can see where she might not trust the police to do a thorough job, especially after the roasting Reynolds gave the capital police department this year over corruption allegations."

"Really?" I made a quick note to check out the security detail and see if any of them were current, retired, or related to any capital police. More work for me, but with all the potential suspects, Irene's defense attorney would be thrilled.

"No, I'm working for Irene O'Donnell and her attorney. She's concerned that she might wind up under the bus given her openly contentious working relationship with the judge."

Judge Beck eyeballed my notepad. "You've color coded it?"

How embarrassing. "It was the only way I could keep everything straight," I confessed. "Highlighted yellow means they had motive. Orange underline means they had substantial motive, in my opinion. Red check mark means I'm fairly certain they would have known about the upstairs bathroom, although if Judge Reynolds had arranged to meet someone there for a private conversation, then he might have told them where it was."

"And the blue?"

"That's if they were unaccounted for during the window I'm assuming the murder to be in." I tossed the notepad onto the table in frustration. "This would be a lot easier if I actually had access to the police notes and evidence. I'm guessing if Irene actually gets arrested her attorney will get those and pass them along. Until then I'm kind of in limbo with almost one hundred suspects, not including the security guards, and no real way to whittle the list down."

"Well, you can take yourself off the list." The judge grinned, lowering himself into a chair next to me.

"Maybe not." I wiggled my eyebrows. "I could have killed him then called you upstairs to act as my alibi."

"First, you didn't even know Judge Reynolds before the party, and I doubt he would have done anything in the half hour you spent talking to him to drive you into a murderous rage. Secondly, there is no way you could have bludgeoned a man to death and walked out of that restroom with your white dress just as pristine as if you'd just picked it up from the cleaners."

"Ah, you must not have noticed that barbeque sauce from the shrimp I somehow managed to drip on myself."

He leaned forward, resting his elbows on the table. "Liar. That dress fit you like a glove. There is nowhere a drop of barbeque sauce, wine, or blood could have hidden that I wouldn't have seen it."

My breath strangled in my throat because that sounded very intimate, very…sexy. I knew he'd thought I'd looked "nice" in the dress, but hadn't realized that he'd taken quite so much notice of every single inch of me in that perfectly fitting gown.

"Maybe I wore a garbage bag over my dress to keep it clean." I laughed, and it sounded more breathless than I'd intended.

He laughed as well, and the pair of us dissolved into near hysterics at the thought of me with several Hefty Lawn and Leaf bags taped over my formal gown, Ziploc bags protecting my shoes as I whacked a grown man to death with a…something heavy.

"We shouldn't be laughing like this," I clapped a hand over my mouth. "A man has been murdered."

"But it's so funny," the judge insisted. "You in your plastic bags, lying in wait for Reynolds to enter the restroom. Springing out to surprise him from a stall and killing him with the toilet tank lid."

My laughing ended abruptly. "How'd you know it was a toilet tank lid?"

Judge Beck shrugged. "If I were going to kill someone in a restroom, a toilet tank lid would certainly do the job. Do you know how heavy those things are? Just try to wrestle one off in a hurry when a toilet is overflowing, and you'll realize what a great weapon they'd be in a pinch."

He'd had the same line of thought I had. I was already wondering how the killer could have left the restroom without dripping blood all over the carpet and the doorway, plus how they'd managed to blend into the party crowd with blood on their tux or uniform. Now I was also wondering how a killer with blood-covered clothing had managed to carry a blood-covered toilet tank lid down a hallway with beige carpet. And where the heck the killer would have stashed such an unwieldy murder weapon?

I sighed, once more thinking that there were too many unknown variables in this whole thing. Which was a good thing for Irene, but a bad thing for those of us wanting to bring Rhett Reynolds' killer to justice.

"So what are *you* working on tonight?" I glanced at the overflowing box and grimaced.

"This is more of a long-term project." He patted the box. "Issues that are likely to come before the appellate court this next year. I know I'm not in the running, but it's good to be prepared in case any other candidates wind up murdered in a restroom. Besides, I want to be able to knowledgably discuss these cases if I need to."

"Don't you have a paralegal to read all these and type up summaries for you?" I teased.

"Yes, but she has an actual full-time job working for me at the courthouse, and I don't want to ruin her holiday season by making her read all these cases. Besides, I've always been the sort of judge who likes to read the original rulings and make my decisions on those rather than on someone else's summary."

I looked at the box and wondered about Judge Beck's holiday season. But the kids were with Heather until Christmas Eve. That gave him plenty of time to pull some late nights and power through what looked to be excruciatingly technical papers. I wasn't exactly one to point fingers given that it was past midnight and I was still up and working. Seemed both of us were going to be pulling all-nighters, just like back in college.

My mind suddenly skipped back to memories of Eli and me studying side-by-side. The early years of our marriage had been hard—me working at the bottom of the hierarchy in a newsroom and him either at school, at the hospital, or with his nose in a book as he threw himself into his studies and residency.

Eli had always been dedicated to his career. It was the mistress, and I was more than willing to step aside for the time he spent in the office, in the surgical suite, researching, and reading. It made him who he was. His passion for his career was just as much a part of the man I loved as his brown eyes and his sideways smile.

"So who are you thinking for the Reynolds murder?" Judge Beck asked as he began to pull stacks of paper from the box.

"Heck if I know. There's Helen Dixon who quite likely orchestrated something with Judge Reynolds to facilitate a quick and profitable divorce from her husband. That leaves the husband as a suspect."

Judge Beck shrugged. "I've known Stuart professionally for five or six years. He's ruthless. I won't say he's not capable of murder, but I see him more as the hiring-a-hitman type."

"Unless he didn't have time to hire a hitman and needed to act fast," I replied. "There's all this other stuff I can't untangle about the Cresswell case. Seems like everyone was involved in that—Dixon, Barnes, Magoo, and Reynolds. It was a long time ago, but I wonder if something surfaced about that."

"That was before my time. I was in law school when it was settled, so I read quite a lot about it, but the actual case-work began almost ten years prior to the settlement. These class action cases take forever to resolve."

"What were your thoughts on it?" I glanced over at the window where the dollar sign had been. "Anyone make out like a bandit in that case? Anything odd you remember about it?"

The judge sat down opposite me. "Everyone made out like bandits in that case besides the plaintiffs. That's the way those things work. By the time the settlement gets divided, all the plaintiffs make a few hundred at the most. The lawyers get a cut of each settlement, so the firms with the most plaintiffs made the most money."

"And that gets divided among the attorneys who worked on the case?" I asked.

Judge Beck nodded. "Firms do it differently, but usually there's a percentage scale depending on if you're a lawyer or a paralegal, and how much time you devoted to the case and gathering the clients. I never worked on any class action lawsuits, but I know once it looks like there's enough evidence to either get a win or a settlement, everyone goes crazy trying to locate and sign on affected plaintiffs."

I frowned. "But that dilutes how much of the settlement each person gets."

The judge shrugged. "Yes, but the more plaintiffs a firm has, a larger percentage of the settlement goes through the firm, and the larger a fee the firm can collect. It's all about the money."

Once more I looked over at the window, and at the ghost in the corner of the room.

"How about Irene O'Donnell?" Judge Beck added. "I know she's retained your services, but do you think she might have done it?"

I sighed. "I'll admit there's a lot of circumstantial evidence against her. She admits her prints are in the restroom. She doesn't have an alibi because she evidently went up to her office on the third floor to throw up and not pass out in front of the partners of the law firm. She was vocal about her dislike of Judge Reynolds. In spite of that I can't see her as the murderer. She was drunk. I'm pretty sure if she'd swung a toilet tank lid at someone, she would have fallen flat on her face and not even hit him."

"Just keep her in the back of your mind, and don't be too hasty about crossing her off your suspect list," the judge told me. "People lie, and those with an agenda and a lot to lose tend to lie a lot."

It sounded a lot like the strange advice Sonny Magoo had given me the night of the party. He'd said not to believe everything that I heard, that some people had their own agendas and were motivated to lie.

Could Irene be lying and using me to cover her tracks? Or was there something else going on here between all these judges whose paths had been intertwined for decades?

CHAPTER 11

*A*fter sending out the skip traces and getting J.T. the summaries of the background checks I'd done, I sat down with Molly and went over the work I needed her to do for the day. Justine and I were supposed to have lunch today, so I skipped out of the office at eleven, hoping to meet with Horace Barnes beforehand.

As luck would have it Horace was in the office along with Damien Smith. Thankfully Damien saw me at the receptionist desk, otherwise I was pretty sure Horace might have insisted I make an appointment for some time in January.

"Hey, there's our new marketing manager!" Damien announced, shaking my hand and leading me past the receptionist to his office. "Glad you decided to join us, Kay. Pierson's loss is our gain."

"Sorry to let you know I'm still working with J.T. I was hoping to talk to Horace if he's available. I've got a few questions about the Cresswell case."

"Whoa, that's ancient history—almost as ancient as Horace himself," Damien joked. The man made a hard left at the office he'd been about to enter, an led me down another hallway. "You're going to need to talk to him about that one. He's the one that managed the plaintiffs for our firm, and it was before my time anyway. Dad might have been able to tell you something about it, but he died last year."

"Oh, I'm so sorry. My condolences on your loss."

Damien paused outside a closed door. "Thanks. It was a rough year, but he's out of pain now and with Mom. Probably up in heaven teasing her about the roast beef being overcooked." He knocked, then swung open the door without waiting for a reply. "Here's Kay Carrera to pester you some more, Horace."

The look Horace shot his partner was a strange mix of venomous and amused. "I'll get you back for this, Smith. Watch your back."

"I always do." Damien laughed and closed the door on his way out.

I hadn't been invited to sit, but I did so anyway, taking one of the chairs across the desk from the attorney.

"So, what can I help you with, Mrs. Carrera?"

Horace Barnes didn't seem too happy about his offer, but I was going to ignore that.

"Call me Kay. I was wondering if you could answer some questions about the Cresswell class action suit."

He blinked in surprise. "Cresswell? That case was huge. It got Stuart Dixon his county judgeship and ten years later his appellate court position. Magoo as well." Horace Barnes settled back in his chair, a smug expression on his face. "The whole thing put SMS&C on the map, not that they were any small fish before."

"Makes me wonder why Sonny Magoo left them. Wouldn't it have benefitted his career more to stay with the firm that was the lead on the case?" I asked.

Horace snorted. "Are you kidding me? At SMS&C he was a big fish among a whole lot of other big fish. Crum and

Stevens was a gold-plated law firm with a great reputation but they didn't have anyone there that knew jack about class action suits. They threw a ton of money at Magoo to take over the whole thing for them. He's the one that found out which of their clients were entitled to a portion of the settlement, held their hands to get them to sign up, and organized the distribution schedule. The firm took a small cut, but Magoo got pretty much the entire attorney's percentage for himself."

"And Dixon?" I asked.

The lawyer steepled his hands beneath his chin. "Same on his side. He was lead attorney. SMS&C had a huge list of plaintiffs. He probably made half of what Magoo did though since he had to split it with the firm and all the other attorneys and paralegals that worked on the case. Different paths, same end result. Dixon got the fame where Magoo got the money. Dixon got a judge appointment and went right up the ladder where it took Magoo longer. They're probably both about the same as far as net worth goes, and career."

"And what did Reynolds have to do with any of this?" I wondered out loud.

"He was the burr under everyone's saddle, that's what Reynolds was." Horace dropped his hands and leaned forward. "The guy went around poaching plaintiffs as they say. Not only did he work off his own firm's client list, he pretty much went door-to-door. Like Magoo, he was the only one in his firm handling the plaintiffs. Unlike Magoo, he only accepted a flat fee for his work and divided the rest among the plaintiffs he represented. It meant they got more than the others and caused a huge stink when it got out. There was a bunch of noise about excessive fees and how attorneys were parasites sucking every dime out of their clients. Let's just say no one liked Rhett Reynolds. If his clients and that Polefax County hadn't loved him so, and it hadn't been an election year, he would never have been appointed as a judge."

I frowned in thought. "Do you think any of that might have been stirred up again recently?"

I doubted someone was holding a grudge for twenty years and committed that murder. It had seemed a killing of desperation, of anger and a need to act fast—not a carefully thought out plan from twenty years ago.

"I haven't heard anything about it recently." Horace tapped on his desk. "Unless one of the candidates had something in his or her background that had to do with the case. Reynolds was the sort of guy who'd feel it was his duty to bring it to light if he discovered someone up for the appellate court position was bribing someone, or taking kickbacks, or had embezzled."

I ran through the list of candidates in my head. Judge Beck was way too young to have been involved in the case. Elaine Stallman and Trent Elliott were of an age that they may have been an assisting attorney. And then there was the man in front of me now....

"Did you handle the plaintiffs for Smith, Barnes & Dorvinski?"

"You betcha. We didn't have many, but someone had to manage the plaintiffs for the firm and I drew the short straw." He shot me a perceptive glance. "Trust me, what I made was peanuts and we kept meticulous financial records. Even had them audited. We specialize in inheritance issues, trust funds, cases involving land titles, and large-scale insurance fraud. We've got wealthy old clients whose families have been with us for generations. I'm not about to ruin a good thing by trying to weasel an extra ten grand out of a class action suit."

It made sense, and I got the impression Horace Barnes was telling the truth. I kept thinking of the ghost's insistence this was about money, and the weird conversation Sonny Magoo had with me at the party.

I stood, then hesitated. "One more thing, if you don't mind—how well do Stuart Dixon and Sonny Magoo get along?"

Harold shrugged. "Like two sharks in a tank. They respect each other. They hang around each other because if one scents blood, the other wants to be right behind him. They'd stab each other in the back if they needed to, but there's never been a need. So basically they get along pretty much like any other two lawyers."

I mulled over that on my way to meet Justine for lunch. She'd picked the location and I was expecting her to suggest an elegant downtown restaurant or a country club, not a little Thai place in an out-of-the-way strip mall. With a name of Tom's Thai, I didn't have high hopes for the food, but I didn't think Justine would suggest something horrible, so I parked and headed into the surprisingly packed restaurant.

Justine waved me down from where she'd grabbed a booth. I slid onto a red vinyl bench seat and took the menu she slid to me.

"Get the papaya salad," she urged. "Their panang is really good, and the eggplant with the black bean sauce is to die for."

I took her advice, choosing the curry over the eggplant dish, then the pair of us settled in to talk about our cats and the upcoming holiday.

"I feel so bad for Judge Reynolds' daughter." Justine made a sympathetic clucking noise. "To lose a parent at Christmas is especially hard. They probably already had gifts for each other and plans for the holiday."

I winced remembering Ruby's comment about the tofu turkey. I needed to give her a call and see if she'd like to join us for the holiday.

"I keep thinking about the murder," Justine continued. "I know Judge Reynolds was a controversial character, but I can't imagine anyone being angry enough to kill him. And how could the murderer have possibly gotten away with the building locked down tight with security? He must have had blood on him. And they interviewed all of us including the catering staff, security, and the musicians. Someone must have had blood splatter on them."

I nodded. "I was wondering the same thing. And how the heck did they get out of the bathroom without dripping blood on that carpet in the hallway? Not to be gruesome, but Judge Reynolds hadn't been dead for long when I found him. I'm guessing the killer attacked him no more than five or ten minutes before my arrival."

"Maybe the killer works there and hid in his or her office until the police left," Justine suggested.

I shook my head. "The police went off an attendee list, checking off who they were interviewing. And I'm pretty sure they searched the building."

She shrugged. "It's an eight-story building. That's a lot of searching to check every office."

"A judge was murdered," I pointed out. "I don't think they'd take short cuts on investigating this one."

"So that means the murderer cleaned up before coming downstairs," she mused.

"He might have done a fast clean-up in the restroom before leaving, then a more thorough clean-up elsewhere. Maybe he wiped off his clothes, washed his face and hands, then went to another restroom?" I frowned. "But I still think there would have been bloody footprints leading to the door and on the carpet. It's like he left through ceiling, or did an Alice in Wonderland thing and went through the mirror."

Our food arrived and we both dug in. The curry was amazing, and I quickly decided this needed to be a place I came to again. Maybe I'd bring Judge Beck here one night. I wondered if the kids liked Thai food.

"Maybe the killer did go through the mirror," Justine mused once we'd finished. "There used to be a door on that wall into the office next door, you know."

I thought for a moment about the remodeling work Eli and I had done on our house. "The opening in the wall framing would probably still be there, but they would have drywalled over it. I can't see the killer taking time to bust through the drywall to hide. Besides, there would have been drywall chunks and dust everywhere."

"I'll bet they didn't even drywall over the door," Justine scoffed. "Under all the gilt and marble, Sullivan is cheap as they come. It's all show with him. Spend money on the trappings, then sweep the rest under the carpet where no one can see it."

My pulse sped up. "You think he just slapped that huge mirror over the door? And put something in front of it on the other side, like a bookcase?"

The judge's wife nodded. "I can completely see him doing something like that."

If that were the case, the killer could have easily slipped into the next office to clean up, or even to get away without leaving bloody footprints outside the restroom door. Plus, that gave me another idea.

"I wonder if Judge Reynolds knew about the door, and if he was actually searching for something in the office, just using the restroom as a means to enter without having to deal with a locked door."

"Could be, although someone must have told him about it because he never worked for SMS&C." Justine sipped her tea, a thoughtful expression on her face. "You know, Trent Elliott has that adjoining office."

"And Trent Elliott is a candidate for the appellate court position."

Justine sat back in the booth. "I've got an idea. Can you get off work tomorrow and join me for lunch in the capital?"

I remembered our dwindling workload. "Sure. I'll need to go into the office first thing to make sure Molly is set for the day, but then I'm sure I can take off."

"Perfect." She grinned. "We're going to take a little field trip, Kay. It's time for us old ladies to do a bit of snooping."

CHAPTER 12

"*H*ere's our plan." Justine rubbed her hands together. "I hope you don't mind, but I enlisted Jorge in our caper."

My eyes grew wide, because I certainly hadn't told Judge Beck that Justine and I were planning to break into an office in a prominent law firm.

She waved her hand. "Oh, I didn't tell him that part. I just said I needed a reason to go to SMS&C today, and that I wanted a reason for them to have us upstairs waiting for a while unattended."

That didn't allay my fears one bit. "And he didn't ask why?"

She grinned. "Jorge has learned never to ask why. The plan is this: we're going to SMS&C to pick up some files Jorge requested from Trent Elliott. Trent has meetings until four, so he's expecting a courier then."

I shook my head, not understanding.

"We're showing up at noon, when Trent is in his meetings and the files won't be ready. Everyone will panic and they'll stick us in a conference room while they try to figure out what files I'm there to get. It will give us time to do our investigative work."

"But your husband is a district court judge. Not to be rude or anything, but unless Trent Elliott has clients that might involve misdemeanors, traffic court, civil cases, or domestic violence, I can't see his staff getting into a panic over not having files ready. They'll just tell us to come back at four, or that they'll courier them over later."

"Trent does handle the occasional civil case as well as landlord/tenant disputes with large apartment complexes, but that's not why people jump when Jorge picks up the phone." Justine's smile was downright impish. "His family has money. He went to Harvard Law. He clerked with a supreme court justice. He knows people, and one phone call can put a stumbling block in someone's career. Not that he'd do it, but they don't know that."

I blinked at her in surprise, immediately wondering why her husband's name wasn't on the list of candidates for the appellate court opening.

Justine laughed. "I know what you're thinking. He doesn't want it. He loves working at the county level, deciding cases first-hand. He loves his job and has absolutely no interest in climbing the judicial or political ladder. It's not like he needs the money, and what he lacks in ambition, his sister more than makes up for."

Hers was a better plan than any I'd come up with. Worst case scenario, we end up spending the afternoon doing a courier job for Judge Sanchez. Best case scenario, we find evidence in the office adjacent to the bathroom that might help the police find the real murderer.

Actually, worst case scenario we get caught snooping in an office that we broke into and get thrown out, although from what Justine had just said about her husband's connections, I doubted that would happen. We'd just end up with a babysitter while they found the files, and we'd find it near impossible to attempt our caper again.

So we better make this work.

We got into Justine's zippy little sports car and headed into the capital. I had a strong sense of déjà vu as we passed in front of the eight-story building and parked in the lot in a spot marked for guests and clients.

"This is the most excitement I've had in five years," Justine whispered as we entered the building. "And that includes the time Jorge agreed to take Salsa lessons with me."

I couldn't imagine the couple burning up the dance floor with their sexy moves, but what did I know? We opened the doors to the office building and entered the atrium which seemed absolutely enormous without a hundred people crammed into it. Our shoes clacked on the marble floor, echoing around the cavernous room. A security guard watched us as we approached the receptionist desk and wrote our names in the visitor's log.

"I'll need to see identification and know who it is you're visiting." The receptionist's crimson lips widened in a smile, but she was clearly assessing us and making a quick judgement about how much bowing and scraping she'd need to do.

The pair of us fumbled in our purses for our licenses. Justine got hers out first.

"Justine Sanchez to see Trent Elliott." Justine's voice was cool with a disinterested superiority. "I'm picking up some files for my husband, Judge Sanchez."

The magic words made the receptionist up the wattage on the smile. She gave Justine's license the barest glance, then handed it back before looking at mine. I considered dropping Judge Beck's name, but decided against it, figuring "landlady" wouldn't garner the same respect as "spouse".

"We were on our way to lunch when Jorge called," Justine

added. "Kay was kind enough to agree to this detour. Hopefully it won't take long."

"Of course, of course." The receptionist handed me back my license, her head bobbing so vigorously it looked as if it might fall off her neck. She picked up her phone and dialed, her fingers beginning to tap nervously on the desk. With an apologetic glance, she dialed another number.

"Martha," she hissed. "Where's Mr. Elliott? I've got Judge Sanchez's wife down here to pick up some files."

I didn't hear was the response was, but the receptionist looked close to panic. Justine looked at her watch and sighed, shaking her head with an expression of mild disgust.

"Okay. Okay. I'll do that. Lunch. They were headed to lunch. Yes." The receptionist hung up the phone, her wide smile strained. "It seems Mr. Elliott is still in his eleven o'clock meeting. His assistant, Martha Wicks, would like to provide you both with some prosecco and antipasto while she locates the files for you." She fumbled for a pair of visitor's passes. "Please take the elevator behind the stairs to the second floor, then take the first hallway to your right to the conference room. Martha will meet you there with refreshments while you wait. I promise it won't be long."

We took the visitors' passes, and Justine sighed once more. "I was hoping he would just bring the files down to us. This is so inconvenient."

I nodded sympathetically. "The club will hold our reservations. I don't mind waiting a bit, Justine. I know how important your husband's work is."

Hopefully that wasn't too over-the-top. I wasn't used to hobnobbing with the rich and politically powerful. Yes, Eli had been a surgeon, and we'd been on our way to probably more wealth than any of these judges, but we hadn't had political clout, and we'd never run in these country club circles either. Even if Eli hadn't been in the accident that changed both our lives, I doubt we *ever* would have run in the country club circles. Eli was too busy with his career and social climbing wasn't his thing. Mine either, although I was getting a kick out of this whole charade.

Justine and I headed for the elevator, chatting about the weather and some charity event that I wasn't sure was a real thing or not. As soon as we got into the elevator, Justine began to giggle.

"Not bad for the daughter of a Filipino seamstress and a Mexican convenience store owner, huh?"

"Seriously?" I chuckled. "My dad was a cop and Mom was a homemaker."

She smiled, as if the memories were fond ones. "They met in New York City, and we lived there until I was seventeen. Five of us in an efficiency in Queens the size of a closet. The few nights when my father wasn't working, he'd cook and the whole floor would be filled with the most amazing smells. Summer evenings we'd open the windows and I'd fall asleep to the sound of the sirens and traffic. Don't get me wrong, small town living has some perks, but I miss the city with all the hustle and bustle. And I truly miss Dad's cooking."

The elevator opened onto the second floor and I had no time to ask her about whether her parents were still alive or still in New York. Justine the judge's wife was back, and we walked down the hallway as if we owned the place, halting long before the conference room where, no doubt, Martha was frantically getting food and bubbly together while trying to reach her boss.

I slowed a step by the restroom but kept going. Office first, because it would be a whole lot easier explaining us being in a restroom than in a private office.

Justine pulled two metal pieces from her pocket and with a quick poke and twist, the door was open.

"I don't want to know who taught you that," I murmured.

"Learned myself." She ducked inside the office then motioned for me to follow, softly closing the door behind us. "Jerk of a landlord up in Queens was always changing the locks if we were a day late on rent. Totally illegal, but bullies like that don't care. Everyone in my family can pick a cheap door lock in less than a second. I've got no idea how to do the expensive electric ones, but these interior office door locks are stupidly simple."

It was a good skill to have. I made a mental note to invite Justine to our Friday night happy hour on the porch events, and to introduce her to Daisy and the others. She'd absolutely fit in with my friends.

The office was spacious with a huge window overlooking the street, a giant mahogany desk complete with a cushy executive chair and gold-plated desk accessories. Three bookshelves were on the wall that adjoined the restroom, and what I assumed was a closet door on the opposite wall along with six tall filing cabinets. The room was painted a light gray with several framed abstract prints strategically placed on the walls. The floor was that expensive vinyl that looks like oak, a gray and white checked area rug under where the guest chairs sat.

On a hunch I went to the desk, pulling a pair of surgical gloves out of my purse and using them to keep any of my fingerprints from getting on the desk drawers as I pulled them open.

"Looks like I'm not the only one with a larcenous past," Justine joked.

"I learned everything I know from episodes of CSI." As I pulled out one of the bottom drawers, I motioned to Justine. "Check this out."

She looked over my shoulder at the brand-new white shirts in the drawer. "Oh, they all do that. Sometimes they work through the night and just freshen up for the next day, or they'll need to put a new shirt on because they dribbled mustard down their front during lunch. Jorge has some stashed at work. I'll bet there's a few suits in the closet as well."

I shut the drawer and went to the closet, using my gloves once more to turn the handle. Sure enough, inside were two suits—one charcoal and the other black, and a pair of men's dress shoes. I scanned the black pants for any blood stains and couldn't see any in the dim light of the closet. What I did find was a dry cleaning tag attached to the jacket, but not the pants.

There were plenty of innocent reasons a man might get his jacket dry cleaned but not his pants on the same suit. There was also one not-so-innocent reason. Someone trying to save money might decide the pants might not require cleaning, but Trent Elliott wasn't the sort who would need to be worrying over a few extra dollars. For a man who wore suits every day, grabbing the set made more sense than leaving the pants behind.

I frowned, thinking for a moment. What would I do if I were the killer? Assuming I removed my jacket downstairs, followed Rhett Reynolds upstairs and caught him snooping... Blood would be on my shirt and pants, and probably my shoes. I'd pop into my office, change pants and shirt, hope the bow tie wasn't blood-splattered, then put on my clean jacket once I was back downstairs. If I didn't have shoe-shine products in my office, I could use my bloody pants to wipe my shoes off, or even change to a pair I had in the closet, then rejoin the party.

Of course, that all depended on having a way to get into my office without tracking blood through the hallway carpet.

Making a beeline to the wall the office shared with the bathroom, I began to examine the bookshelves, hoping one would swing out just like a secret entrance on Scooby Doo, and reveal a door to the bathroom. That's when I saw something that made the hair rise on my neck.

"Look at this," I whispered to Justine as I knelt down and pulled out my cell phone. There, at the edge of a bookcase, was a bit of red, on the floor. It was barely noticeable, and if I hadn't been examining the bookshelves for secret passageways, I never would have noticed it.

"Is it blood?" Justine frowned. "Maybe we should call the police."

"Check out the scuff marks and indentations on the floor," I went on. "This bookshelf wasn't always here. I'd say it was about a foot to the left. And these books are all clean, the shelf dusted where the other shelves aren't."

None of them were obviously dirty. It was the faint sort of dust that builds up over a couple of weeks when the cleaning service only does the bare minimum. This shelf had more books on it than the others, and there were spots on the other bookcases where it looked like books had recently been removed.

I tried to be careful as I hurriedly removed books from the one bookcase and put them into the others. Then I scooted it aside to reveal where the drywall ended and a door began."

"Bingo," I said in a hushed voice.

"We're taking too long," Justine mentioned softly. "That Martha is going to come hunt us down in five, so hurry it up, girl."

I ran my fingers down the edge of the door but didn't find a doorknob. Of course, they would have removed it when they converted the restroom from private to office use. I thought it was funny that they hadn't bothered to drywall over the door, but I guess a budget was a budget.

"I think that mirror is on the other side of this," I

commented. "Does it swing out or in? I'm guessing it opens into the restroom, otherwise Judge Reynolds wouldn't have been able to get in the office without pushing the bookshelf over."

Rhett Reynolds was no slacker, but he didn't look like he'd be able to push a heavy wood bookcase, even one without a whole lot of books on it, aside. Or would he? I grabbed the edge of the bookcase and tugged, surprised at how easily it moved. Was it on casters? Or maybe it wasn't solid wood after all?

Moving the bookcase revealed a hole where the door-knob had once been. I reached through and felt something hard on the other side. The mirror, I was guessing.

"Hurry up!"

For the first time I was hearing a bit of fear in Justine's voice. I pushed the bookcase back, rushing to replace the books that had been there.

"Let's go," I told Justine. I needed to think about this, and time was not on our side. Hopefully I could work through my mental gyrations while we ate antipasto and drank pros-ecco, because I wasn't sure we'd get another opportunity to examine this office.

We raced for the door, Justine pausing to carefully peek out before giving me the sign that the coast was clear. She clicked the lock on the door before shutting it, and we fast-walked our way down the hall, trying to control our panting as we got to the conference room.

I got the impression that we were five seconds from Martha coming to search for us. For a woman who'd had no advance warning at all, she'd put together a nice spread. Food was laid out on little blue dishes. Tiny plates with tiny silverware and tiny napkins embossed with the law firm's initials were neatly placed in front of two chairs. Bubbly sat open in a silver container filled with ice, a monogrammed cloth around the neck of the bottle. Martha let out a relieved breath and gave us a nervous smile, moving to pour the prosecco.

"I can't believe we ran into John in the hallway," Justine announced. "What a surprise that was."

"He's really aged since I saw him last," I replied. I was catching onto this whole thing. It was like doing improv in theater class back in college.

Justine shrugged. "Well, that's to be expected, dear." She turned to Martha with a smile. "Is this for us? How very nice of you. I hope you can locate those files of Trent's soon, though. We've got reservations at the club. I hate to be more than half an hour late. It's so rude, you know."

I turned a laugh into a cough, and snatched up a glass of prosecco, taking a quick sip. Martha entreated us to enjoy the food and drink, then practically ran out the door. Justine and I took our seats and helped ourselves. It was almost ten minutes on the dot when Martha came dashing in, two files in her arms.

"Mr. Elliott apologizes that he wasn't here to give these to you himself. He says he misunderstood Judge Sanchez and didn't believe they would be picked up until later this afternoon. Again, our sincerest apologies for making you wait."

"Oh, no bother at all." Justine stood and took the files from her, sliding them into her designer tote. "We enjoyed your hospitality here, Martha. I'll make sure I tell my husband how helpful you were, and how you went out of your way to make sure we didn't miss our lunch."

The woman practically glowed, her shoulders relaxing with relief. And then she put a total hitch in our plan by kindly escorting us from the conference room and down the hall. I exchanged a quick glance with Justine, then headed for the restroom.

"Think I should probably stop off here before we head to lunch," I announced as I pushed the door open.

"Oh, good idea." Justine hesitated in the doorway. "Thank you again, Martha. We'll just freshen up a bit, then leave our badges with the receptionist. Have a lovely day!"

The door shut as a conflicted expression settled on Martha's face. Poor woman. Hospitality and policy probably dictated that she escort us out, but following us into the restroom and hanging around while we took care of biological and cosmetic matters would be rude and seem as if she didn't trust us.

Luckily Martha didn't follow us in. I waited a few moments as Justine ran some water in the sink and flushed the commode for effect, then I peeked out into the hallway.

No Martha.

"Here," I pulled more surgical gloves out of my purse and handed a pair to Justine.

"How many of these do you have?" she exclaimed, eyeing my bag as if it a magical device.

"Boxes," I told her. "My husband was a surgeon and he used to bring them home all the time. They were handy for when we were redecorating the house—painting or staining furniture. Eli always liked to wear them when he was cleaning chicken or patting out hamburgers and joke about how the kitchen was just another surgical suite."

She tilted her head. "Husband? I just assumed you and Nathaniel..."

I focused on forcing my fingers into the gloves, remembering how Eli used to put them on and pull them off as if he did it dozens of times every day. Which, of course, he did.

"Eli passed in February this year. We had this huge Victorian in Locust Point and it was a bit much for me on my own, both space-wise and financially. Judge Beck needed somewhere for him and the kids during his divorce process, and I needed a tenant if I was planning on keeping the house."

Justine stood there, gloves still balled up in her hands. "You didn't know him before he moved in?"

"No, not at all. I mean, I'd heard his name as a circuit court judge, but I'd never met him personally. My husband was in a bad accident ten years ago about the time he and his family moved to the area. We might have met socially here and there if I hadn't been focusing on the care of my husband, but maybe not. Eli wasn't much of a golfer, and neither of us were the country club types."

I could feel Justine's eyes on me as I walked over to the mirror, carefully examining the gilt trim.

"He's a good man, you know," she said, her voice casual. "Kind of old fashioned in some ways, but honest, kind, and loyal. If he thinks of you as a friend, then you can count yourself lucky. If he thinks of you as more than a friend, as family, then you can count yourself more than lucky."

"I definitely think of him and his children as family." I hooked my fingers on the mirror to peek behind it and nearly fell over when it swung open.

There was the door with the round hole where the knob had been. I gave it a gentle push and heard it bump against the bookshelf. With a slightly harder push, I felt the shelf move a bit on the casters.

I didn't want to do anything more, afraid that I'd dislodge the shelf or books to a point that Trent would be tipped off that someone was snooping in his office, or had discovered the old washroom door.

He'd taken a huge risk that the police wouldn't search the office adjacent to the restroom, but I was sure he hadn't expected Reynolds' body to be discovered so soon. And he was no doubt confident that the police wouldn't do more than dust the mirror for prints, and perhaps test the handle on his office door to make sure it was locked. He would have had time to dispose of the bloody clothes and shoes, and to make sure any trace of blood in his office was gone. And he'd done that, except for that bit of blood by the edge of the bookshelf.

I replaced the mirror and turned to Justine. "I wonder what Judge Reynolds would have been looking for in Trent's office?"

Justine shrugged. "Whatever it was, I'm guessing Trent didn't want him to find it. Or if he found it, Trent didn't want him to tell anyone about it."

Judge Beck had said that Reynolds wasn't a contender for the appellate court position, in spite of his nomination. Trent Elliott, on the other hand, was a serious contender. The only motive I could think of for Reynolds to be snooping in Trent's office, or for Trent to kill Judge Reynolds, was because he'd found something that could ruin the other man's chances at the promotion. Or possibly ruin his career altogether.

I wondered if Ruby had gone through the things in her father's house yet. Did Judge Reynolds have anything there on his computer or in his files about what he had on Trent Elliott?

Not that it mattered at this point. Murder would probably put Trent Elliott in jail for a whole lot longer than whatever else he'd done in his past. And a crime in the hand was definitely worth two in a deceased man's house.

CHAPTER 13

*J*ustine and I actually did have lunch at the club. It seems that my new friend never joked around when it came to food. That's how we found ourselves discussing our next steps while eating Cobb salads and drinking perfectly sweetened iced tea.

"It has to be him," I insisted between bites of salad. "Reynolds was getting something out of his office, using the door behind the mirror."

"But how did he know about the door behind the mirror?" Justine pointed her fork at me for emphasis. "If he wanted something out of Trent's office, why didn't he just pick the lock like I did? Or get a master key."

"I don't know the answers to those questions, not yet anyway." I frowned in thought. "What I do know is that Reynolds was in the restroom for a reason, and I doubt it had to do with any biological necessity. He was near the mirror, because the pool of blood was against that wall. There was no sign of any drops of blood leaving out that bathroom doorway, or anything on that beige carpet in the hall."

"Maybe the killer cleaned up before leaving the restroom," Justine suggested.

"Where would he have stashed his clothing? He must have had a way out of that restroom that didn't involve going out the door. Trent's office has vinyl flooring. He's got a change of clothing. It would have been easy for him to go through, change, do a quick clean-up, then be back downstairs before anyone knew he was gone."

"I still have doubts about Reynolds knowing the existence of the door behind the mirror. And there are a lot of holes in this Trent theory. If the blood was against the wall, maybe it seeped under the secret door and that's how it got on the office floor. Maybe none of this had to do with the door or Trent. Maybe the killer…I don't know, maybe he wasn't at the party. Maybe he came in from outside the building, killed Judge Reynolds in the bathroom, then put some plastic bags on his feet and managed to leave without leaving any blood trace."

"The police would have checked the door security logs as well as entrance cameras. It had to have been someone at the party, and my money is on Trent." I knew exactly what Justine was saying. And the more we talked, the more my enthusiasm fell.

She was right. I didn't know why Reynolds was in that bathroom. I didn't know why anyone would have wanted to kill him. And my whole theory about the mirror door and the change of clothing was nothing but a theory based on less than circumstantial evidence.

Suddenly this Cobb salad tasted like cardboard. I'd taken a whole day off work for this. I'd chased down my silly fantasies. I'd involved my new friend in something that quite a few law enforcement officials might consider breaking and entering. Yeah, Justine and I had fun, but in the end, I was an amateur, a newly minted private investigator tilting at windmills.

"I'll call the detective on the case and give her a heads' up on this whole thing," Justine said, spearing a forkful of salad. "I figure it would be less suspicious coming from me than you, given that you were the one who discovered the body. I wouldn't want them thinking you were snooping around, trying to solve this case behind their backs."

The last was delivered with a wink. I understood her reasoning, but I wasn't sure what she intended to tell the police, so I asked her.

"Just that I was at the office today to pick up some files, and when I was using the restroom on the way out, I accidently moved the mirror and noticed there was a door behind it leading into the adjacent office."

I choked back a laugh. "Oh, because *that* sounds so believable. They'll think you were in the restroom out of some morbid sense of curiosity, and that you were ransacking the place looking for clues."

Justine shrugged. "So they think a judge's wife got nosy while running an errand for her husband. They're not going to scold me or anything, especially when I tell them I found a secret doorway their crime scene folks somehow missed."

"True." I nodded thoughtfully. "But I thought you'd decided this theory was all hooey."

"Maybe. Maybe not. Either way I think the police should know. We were only in that office a few minutes. Maybe they can shine blue lights on stuff and find blood traces we missed, or find the bloody clothing hidden up in the ceiling tiles or something."

She had a point. We could lob this all over to the police and let them apply their expertise. If it turned out that I was right, then I could feel a little bit of vindication as well as satisfaction in my newly licensed investigative skills. If not, well no harm except for a waste of some police time.

* * *

"YOU AND JUSTINE DID WHAT?" Judge Beck ran a hand through his blond hair, making it stand on end. I eyed him, thinking that if Madison saw him right now, she wouldn't think her father looked so staid.

"Nosed around the restroom where Judge Reynolds died." I winced. "And we looked around the office next door."

"Which was unlocked."

He'd said that like it was a statement. I knew this was one of those "I don't want to know" things, but too bad.

"No. Justine picked the lock."

The judge let out a long breath and ran a hand through his hair once more.

"But look." I turned my phone for him to see the breaking news headlines. "The police were able to use the information that we—I mean Justine—gave them, and they took Trent in for questioning."

Judge Beck took the phone from my hand. "All this because you and Justine snooped around and found a door between the office and the restroom?"

He and I both knew that wouldn't be enough to bring Trent in for questioning. Actually I was doubting anything we'd found would be enough to bring Trent in for questioning.

"The police must have found more than we did," I told him.

"And what exactly *did* you find?"

Here's where I told him my wild theory and all the shaky circumstantial evidence to support it.

"When Justine first told me about that restroom at the

party, she'd said it used to be an executive washroom. I didn't remember it until later, but if it was an executive washroom, then the door to the hall was added later, and there would have been a door leading to one of the adjoining offices. I remembered thinking it was weird that there was no blood trace I could see leaving the washroom or out on that beige hallway carpet, and wondered if the door to the office was still there."

The judge nodded. I went on to tell him about what looked like a bit of blood on the office floor by the bookshelf, about the pants hanging in the closet. I went over my entire theory while he fixed me with that stern, attentive, flat stare I imagined he presented to prosecutors and defense attorneys.

I was sweating with anxiety when I finished, and neither my career nor my client depended on the judge's decisions. I had no idea how attorneys faced this man in the courtroom and didn't wind up having a panic attack.

"If there was a door under that full-length mirror, then there was enough of a space at the threshold for blood to have seeped into the office from the crime scene," he commented.

I wiped a bead of sweat from my forehead. "I know. That's a possibility."

"Trent rearranging his bookshelf or dry cleaning his jacket without the pants aren't exactly incriminating," he added.

"I know, but it makes sense that the killer knew about that doorway, that Judge Reynolds knew about that doorway. If he'd used it to gain access to Trent's office to find something incriminating, and Trent caught him leaving through the doorway, then it's logical to think Trent would have killed him to hide the evidence, and changed his clothes before heading back down to the party."

Even as I said it, it sounded implausible.

"But why kill Reynolds? Snooping isn't exactly a rock-solid motive for murder." He must have seen the look on my face, because the judge stepped close to me, putting his hands on my arms. "Kay, I've seen your deductive skills at work. I've seen how thorough you are in your investigations. I know this is you thinking things through, discussing possibilities out loud, but don't jump the gun on this. Don't go to the police unless you have enough proof to back up your ideas. And please, for the love of God, don't go breaking into offices. Or buildings. Or cars."

He was right, and I was a bit ashamed of myself for racing ahead on such shaky evidence. I knew better than this. If I'd submitted this story back in my journalism days, I would have been fired. Not enough proof. Not anywhere near enough proof.

But then why had the police taken Trent in for questioning?

CHAPTER 14

*T*rent was out of the police station almost as fast as he went in, making me wonder if they truly were just questioning him and not considering him a suspect. Since the whole thing had been splashed all over the news last night, I wasn't shocked to see a press conference in the morning from Trent Elliott and his lawyer—who did the talking. Trent stood beside the man in an immaculate suit, his dark hair silver at the temples.

It seemed that Trent was horrified to find out that Judge Reynolds' killer had used his office to escape from the scene of the crime. The lawyer went on to say that although he couldn't reveal any details, both Mr. Elliott and the management at Sullivan, Morris, Stein and Callahan were cooperating fully with the police and helping in any way they could to bring the murderer to justice.

At the end of the press conference a few reporters shouted out questions, but the lawyer waved them away and followed Trent Elliot from the stage.

I had a few thoughts as I parked the car and walked into the office. One—that in my opinion, Trent Elliott looked weak having his lawyer deliver the press conference. That was fine for a regular defendant, but for an attorney who was most likely going to be appointed to the appellate court? The guy should have had enough confidence and oratory skill to speak for himself.

Two—maybe the reason Trent was in and out so quickly was because he might not have even known about the door to the restroom. Yes, he'd been with the firm for a long time, but when *had* that restroom been converted? Maybe I needed to look at people who worked at SMS&C before that had happened.

Maybe I needed to look into who had that office at the time it was converted.

"Look what I have." I held a plastic carrier aloft as I walked through the office door.

"Muffins?" J.T. sniffed the air. "I'm guessing ginger and vanilla?"

"Scones?" Molly squinted, trying to see through the carrier. "Or banana bread?"

"Cookies." I put the container down next to the coffee maker and opened it up. I'd been making cookies all week and storing them. This was a mix of all of them—gingerbread, peanut butter blossom, coconut balls, candy-cane sugar cookies, and chocolate macadamia.

"Cookies?" Molly wrinkled her nose. "For breakfast."

I laughed. "Not much more sugar than muffins, scones, or banana bread. Besides, it's almost Christmas. Cookies for breakfast are part of my holiday tradition."

I left the two of them to descend on the cookies like a pair of piranhas and went to see what we had going on for the day. We were only two days until Christmas, and work was beginning to slow down as people took off early for the holiday. The workload for the day was low enough that Molly could handle it on her own. That would leave me to keep working on the Reynolds case—or rather the Irene O'Donnell case.

J.T. went out to meet with bail bonds clients. I got Molly set up with her work for the day, then called the cell phone number Irene had given me.

"Thought the heat was off me for a moment," she said. "When I saw on the television last night that they'd taken Trent in, I was ready to break out the bubbly."

I told her about the hidden door, the blood by the shelf, and my theory that the killer went through Trent's office to clean up rather than head down the hallway.

"There's a secret door between Trent's office and the restroom? And there was blood in his office?" She let out a muffled curse.

"I don't have access to the police reports, but I definitely know about the door. That restroom used to be an executive washroom connected to Trent's office, and when they converted it for public use, they didn't bother to drywall over the door—or even take it out."

"I didn't know any of this. I've worked there for five years and never knew."

"Do you think Trent knew about the door?" I asked.

"Probably not. I'm thinking if he knew about it he would have insisted the thing be walled over. I mean the idea that someone could get into his office from the restroom would completely freak the guy out."

It was a good point, and made me think once more that maybe the killer was someone who'd been there when the restroom was converted.

"Um, full disclosure here," Irene continued, "my prints are in Trent's office."

"Of course they are. You work there. You were probably in his office—"

"No. My prints are all over his office. Other…stuff too. On the desk, on the floor, on the chairs, up against the wall."

Oh my.

"You and Trent were…."

"Screwing like monkeys. Nothing serious, you know."

Wonderful. "Is there anything else I need to know, Irene?"

"No, but if I think of anything, I'll call."

I hung up and poured myself a coffee, grabbing a couple of chocolate chip cookies. It was time for sugar.

I needed to know when the restroom was converted, and who had Trent Elliott's office at that time, and there was only one person I knew who had quick access to that information and would be happy to share it with me.

Justine.

"Ready for another caper?" Justine asked when I called her. "What office are we breaking into this time? Should I bring a gun?"

A gun? Yikes.

"No breaking and entering this week," I told her. "Actually I'm looking for some information. I need to know when that restroom was converted and who had Trent's office at the time."

"Oh, excellent idea! I remember the restroom was converted around twenty years ago, but I'm not sure the exact year or who had that office. Let me make a bunch of phone calls and get back to you."

I hung up and eyed the few files on my desk. The way things were going, I might actually end up going home early today. There was nothing more I could do on the Reynolds murder until Justine got back to me.

Molly and I went out to lunch together, then we split the remaining skip trace files and finished up around two o'clock.

"If you need the hours you can update the client database and clean up a little," I told her.

"Nah, I'm happy to get home early today." She grinned. "Hunter and I are going to make popcorn balls and wrap gifts."

We locked up, leaving J.T. a note and headed out. I was just starting my car when my phone rang. I wasn't sure whether I was excited or not that Justine was getting back to me so quickly. Part of me really wanted the evening off, but the other part really wanted to dig back into this case.

But it wasn't Justine on the phone, it was Ruby.

CHAPTER 15

"*I* know it's last minute and two days before Christmas, but do you think you could come over and help me go through my father's condo?"

"Of course I can." I just needed to text Judge Beck and ask him to let Taco out and feed him when he got home. I really didn't have anything to do and had planned on spending the evening knitting and cuddling with my cat.

"Thank you so much. I just want to sort through everything and grab anything important or sentimental before I fly out. The police said I can go in now."

"The police searched your father's home?" I wondered if that was part of the murder investigation.

"Well, they had to after the break-in. I'm just glad they were quick because I want to make sure I grab photos and other things."

"Break-in?" I was horrified. As if the woman hadn't already been through enough. First her father is murdered, and now his condo is robbed. And it didn't escape my notice that the two crimes might be connected.

"I went in this morning to get a few things and called the

police right away when I saw. I also called that detective that's working on Dad's murder. She came right out."

Ah yes, Bettie Page. "Do they know when the robbery occurred?"

"His neighbors are out of town. The Eylers snowbird it every year at their place in Florida, and Pete left last Friday to stay with his kids for a few weeks. It could have been any time from Saturday night until last night." Ruby made a frustrated noise. "I wish I'd gone over Sunday. They took his television, computers, hard drives, and USB sticks. The place is a mess."

I knew there were horrible people who watched the obituaries and took advantage of empty homes to rob those who had died, but in spite of the theft of the television, I was sure whoever robbed Judge Reynolds' home was making sure whatever was on those computers, hard drives, and USB sticks didn't come to light. Someone had murdered the man, and that same someone was trying to get rid of the evidence.

Sadly, they probably had gotten rid of the evidence.

"Should I meet you at your father's house or yours?" I asked Ruby.

She gave me the address for her father's place, and I told her I'd meet her there. As I drove, I couldn't help but feel frustrated at how this case had gone so far. Hopefully the police had more than I did and were close to finding the murderer, because all I had was a lot of circumstantial stuff and no real suspect.

Rhett Reynolds' condo *was* a mess. Ruby was already inside with half a dozen boxes and lots of industrial-strength garbage bags. Sadly, there appeared to be more going into the garbage bags than in the boxes.

Whoever had done this, they'd been thorough. Sofas and chairs were slashed and turned over. The drawers had been removed from dressers, the entertainment center, and the desk, the contents dumped out. Drapes and blinds were yanked down and broken. The contents of every kitchen cabinet had been scattered all over the floor, a few of the doors broken off the hinges. I didn't go into the bedroom, but I was pretty sure it had been subjected to the same treatment.

"Oh Ruby, I'm so sorry!" I exclaimed as I surveyed the damage.

"It's okay. Really. Insurance will pay for any damage, and I was going to have to get rid of most of this stuff anyway."

"What can I do?" I picked up an empty garbage bag and began to look around.

"I'm going to save most of the trash-type clean-up for when I get back." Ruby nudged a box over my way. "Only put anything that's clearly broken in the trash bag, and ask if you think something broken might have sentimental value. If you find pictures or anything that looks like it might be valuable, put it in the box."

I got to work, taking pictures out of their smashed frames, and carefully placing them in a box. We talked as we worked, Ruby telling me about her childhood and reminiscing as various knickknacks sparked her memory. We moved into the kitchen, and then into the bedroom as night fell. My stomach was protesting the lack of dinner, but I wasn't about to call a break when I could see how important it was for Ruby to at least sort through the majority of the belongings in this one trip.

When she finally called it quits we had a dozen garbage bags that went into the chute at the end of the hallway, and six rather heavy boxes. It took us three trips to get them all downstairs and into both her tiny car and my old sedan. I followed Ruby to her house, and grabbed a box, heading to her door where I heard Dolly barking and scratching.

"I really appreciate this," Ruby said as she fumbled for her keys. "I'm flying out to Seattle to see my mom tomorrow and didn't want to leave Dad's place in that state."

"You're going to your mom's?" I shifted the weight of my box. "I was going to invite you to join us for Christmas."

"Thank you for that, but I think it's time I started making more of an effort to spend time with Mom. I was always closer to Dad. My mother and I didn't get along very well in my teen or college years, and I kind of let some emotional distance build between us. Dad's death made me realize that we never know how much time we have—or how much our loved ones have. If something happened to Mom, I'd always regret not getting to know her better now that I'm an adult."

Ruby finally got the door open and I went in behind her, trying not to trip over an enthusiastic Dolly.

"My grandfather used to always say that time was the most precious gift we have." I sat my box down near Ruby's little Christmas tree and turned to go get another box when I noticed something. It was a gift wrapped in blue and silver paper, addressed to Ruby.

"That's from Dad." Tears choked her voice. "He gave it to me last week before the party, and I haven't had the courage to open it yet. I'm afraid I'd fall apart into a mess. The last gift he ever gave me."

"Oh, honey." I gave her shoulders a quick hug. "Do you want to open it tonight with me here? Before you fly out? Or do you want to just pack it away and save it for when you feel ready?"

She picked up the box, turning it over in her hands. "I think I *would* like to open it now. Maybe it's something I can take on the flight."

I sat on the floor next to her as she ripped the paper off and opened the box. Inside was a soft, organic cotton hoodie, a YETI mug, and a dark blue, weighted blanket. There was no special card, no note inside to indicate that Rhett

Reynolds might have thought this would be his last Christmas gift to his daughter.

"This is wonderful," she whispered. "Dad always took note of when I said I liked something. These are all the things I wanted, but just couldn't justify spending the money on."

"You can take the mug with you to visit your mother," I told her. "And maybe wear the hoodie. That way it will feel like your dad is close to you."

"That's a great idea, Kay." Ruby stood and took her coat off, putting the hoodie on over her shirt. "It's so soft and warm."

I stood up as well, waited for Ruby to put her coat back on, then we made two more trips to our cars to bring in the rest of the boxes.

"Can I get you something to eat or drink?" Ruby asked once we'd stacked the last of the boxes by her tree.

"It's late. I should be getting back home," I said, glancing at my watch.

"Well, at least let me get you some coffee or hot tea for the road."

It was a good idea. I was actually a little tired from my late nights earlier this week, and some caffeine would do me good. "Coffee would be lovely, thanks."

I hung my coat on the rack next to Ruby's, then went into the kitchen and talked about my Christmas plans as she brewed the coffee. When it was done, she pulled a go-cup out of a cabinet and filled it for me.

She handed me the cup. "Don't worry about getting this back to me. I've got dozens of them from conventions and seminars. The only one that matters to me is the YETI one Dad gave me."

I thanked her again and she accompanied me to the door, holding the coffee as I put my coat back on.

"Call me when you get back," I told her, taking the coffee

back. "We'll get together for lunch and you can tell me about Seattle. I'd be happy to help you do the rest of the clean-up on your father's place, too."

"That would be wonderful." She stuck her hands in the pockets of the hoodie, and an odd expression came over her face. With a slight frown, she pulled something out of the right pocket.

It was a USB stick.

I sucked in a breath, and the pair of us stared at it in wonder.

"Oh, Dad."

"Should we take a look?" I asked her.

She nodded, and once again I took off my coat. As Ruby opened up her laptop and booted it up, I sipped my coffee and wondered what the contents of the little stick would reveal.

It was full of files with names like Cresswell payout 05. There were spreadsheets full of accounting data, and reports showing payouts. It was more than either of us could comprehend at a glance. Ruby copied the contents over to her hard drive, then opened one last document that had her name on it.

My little Gem. I'm so sorry that you're reading this because that means I'm gone. I'm so proud of you. You're my heart and I love you.

Please copy these files and keep the records in a safe place, then turn this over to the police. They'll know what to do with it. And if they decide they want to cover it up because they're too afraid to slay the dragon, then it will be up to you to make things right. Go to the press, but first talk to Helen Dixon. She knows everything.

Love always, Dad

Ruby swallowed a few times and blinked back tears. Then she pulled the USB stick out of her computer and handed it to me. "Can you give this to the detective for me, Kay? I know it sounds horrible, but I don't want to delay my flight, and this needs to go to her first thing in the morning."

"I'll take care of it," I vowed. "You go have a wonderful holiday reconnecting with your mother. When you get back, we'll talk."

She nodded then reached over and gave me a hug. "Thank you. And Merry Christmas, Kay."

"Merry Christmas to you too."

I left Ruby wearing her new hoodie, Dolly sitting by her feet as she watched me start my car and pull out of the driveway. It was a quiet, contemplative drive home as I thought about loss, love, gifts, and family.

I thought about one more thing as well. First thing in the morning, as soon as I'd delivered this USB stick to the police, I was going to go have a chat with Helen Dixon.

CHAPTER 16

*I*t was Christmas Eve Day and we had so little in the way of work that J.T. told Molly and I to go ahead and take off once we were done. I was feeling bad about working this case and leaving Molly with all the skip traces, so I pitched in and we managed to get finished around eleven. I was just about to leave the office when Justine called.

"Got it!" she announced.

"So do I, but you first."

"The executive washroom was converted twenty or twenty-one years ago according to my people in the know. And Stuart Dixon had that office at the time. I'm positive of that because everyone I spoke to remembered him making a huge stink about the firm taking one of his perks from him. Most of the former employees I spoke with didn't know about the door being left on and just covered up, but two did. Those two told me Stuart complained about that as well, saying Sullivan was a cheap you-know-what."

He'd been the lead on the Cresswell case. What if all that

accounting data Rhett Reynolds had accumulated showed he was guilty of fraud or embezzlement?

"Would Dixon's old files still be in that office?" Because if they were, that would definitely be a reason for Reynolds to be up on the second floor.

"Maybe. Those cabinets weigh a ton. There's an off-site company that securely stores the boxes of files, but there might be personal notes and stuff in the filing cabinet."

Would Dixon have been careless enough to leave incriminating evidence behind in his old office file cabinet? I just couldn't see that. And I definitely couldn't see Rhett Reynolds sneaking into an office when the actual files for the case were in a dozen dusty boxes off site somewhere.

"But wait, there's more," Justine quipped. "Evidently it's well known that the office keys are never changed. As in, *never*. So the key Stuart Dixon used to get into his office is the same one Trent Elliot uses now. And the same one probably three other people who had that office used. If he killed Reynolds, and changed clothes in Trent's office, he could have easily gotten the borrowed pants cleaned, come back and switched them for the bloody ones. Except Dixon isn't at all the same size as Trent Elliott. There's no way that man could squeeze into Trent's pants and walk around without the seams splitting."

She did have a point. "Besides, if Dixon killed Reynolds, why not kill his wife? I'm assuming she knew the dirt on him and told Reynolds or vice-versa. That might be why she got a big divorce settlement out of him. But why kill one person and trust the other to keep your secret?"

"So probably not Dixon, but maybe a friend of his? Maybe someone he paid to make sure Reynolds didn't get whatever it was he was looking for?"

I frowned. "No. I don't think this was planned at all. It was a hurried, panicked murder. And Dixon wouldn't have been running around the party at midnight looking to bribe a state senator, judge, or lawyer to immediately run upstairs and off someone."

Justine sighed. "Okay. I'm stumped. What's your news?"

I told her about Rhett Reynolds' condo being burglarized, and what Ruby found in her Christmas present.

"Oooo, that's so exciting! Maybe it *was* Stuart Dixon who did it."

"I don't know. That's why I want to go talk to Helen Dixon right after I swing by the police station. You wouldn't happen to have her phone number and address, would you?"

"I sure would!" Justine rattled off the information. "If she is trying to give you the slip, you call me. She'll listen to me. It's in her best interests to go talk to the police, especially when they figure out exactly what's on that USB stick."

I hung up with a promise to give Justine a call later and let her know what happened, then I headed to the capital.

By the time I reached the police station and parked, it was just after noon. I had no idea if police detectives kept conventional lunch schedules or not. I didn't want to wait around for an hour on Christmas Eve for her to finish her burger and fries, and I really didn't want to give this evidence to anyone aside from the detective working the case. Worried that a few seconds might mean the difference between the detective being at lunch or not, I ran from the parking lot, once again noting that while daily yoga did wonders for my flexibility it did nothing for my cardio fitness.

I made it up to the front desk, still out of breath, and asked for Detective Bettie Page.

"Who?" The young man at the desk scanned a list and slowly shook his head. We don't have any Detective Page here, ma'am."

What the heck was her name? I couldn't believe I'd

forgotten the detective's name, and I couldn't believe this man was so young he didn't know who Bettie Page was.

"I mean Detective…Burger? No. Burlesque? No. Burgess. That's it—Detective Burgess."

The young man shot me a puzzled glance, then looked down again at the directory. "Just one moment, ma'am."

He dialed the number, spoke for a few moments, then winced and looked up at me. "May I ask who is calling?"

Good grief, this poor guy must have just started today. "Kay Carrera. I'm here about the Reynolds case. Please tell her I have some information for her."

He relayed the information, then hung up. "Someone will be right out, ma'am."

I didn't have to wait for long. Detective Burgess came up herself to retrieve me, leading me back to what looked to be the same interview room I'd been in last time—although I'm sure they all looked pretty much the same.

"So what do you have for me, Mrs. Carrera?" she asked once we were seated.

I pulled out the USB drive and told her the story. A small smile twitched at the corner of her mouth. I got the feeling this woman didn't smile very often, and that this was as close to euphoria as she'd most likely ever been in her life.

"And why didn't Miss Reynolds bring this in? Or call us?"

"Because she'd just spent an emotional day going through her father's condo that had been robbed and vandalized, then an emotional evening opening the very last Christmas present he'd ever give her. It was late. She had an early flight to Seattle to spend the holiday with her mother. I think the woman has been through enough, so I offered to bring this in. I'm sure you can reach her on her cell phone, but the woman has been through a lot this week. I'd hope that you'd only contact her if it was urgent and allow her some time to visit with family and grieve."

Detective Burgess blinked at my tone, which I'll admit was a bit combative. I don't know what had gotten into me lately, but I was even more of a protective hen than usual.

"Thank you." She held up the USB stick. "I'll log this into evidence and get our financial folks on it right away. Hopefully there will be something in all these numbers that leads us to the murderer."

If the numbers didn't then the letter to Ruby telling her to talk to Helen Dixon definitely would. It was very bad of me not to tell the detective up front about that, but I wanted to talk to Helen first. I wanted her to be the one offering up what she knew rather than having suspicious police descending on her the day after Christmas.

Thanking the detective, I got up and followed her to the door. Wishing both her and the man at the reception desk a Merry Christmas, I headed to my car and my, hopefully, last appointment of the day—Helen Dixon.

The address Justine had given me was in a waterfront community just outside the capital. Merit Lake was man-made, and a haven for those who loved boating, jet skiing, or just lounging on their docks. I pulled up outside a Colonial-style home that looked to be over four thousand square feet with a fountain in the middle of the circular drive.

After leaving a message before I'd headed out from the police station lot, I managed to reach Helen, who nervously told me to come by her house. I was guessing Justine must have called her and let her know the severity of the situation, because she was waiting at the door as I parked.

"I didn't do it," she said the moment I was within ten feet of her. "I didn't kill him. I had no reason to kill him."

"But you know who did?"

She nodded, then waved me in. I sat in a white and gold upholstered chair, and she sat in the matching one beside me. I looked down at the white carpet, then over at the gold drapes, and wondered if she'd used the same designer as SMS&C.

"Justine called and told me, and I just don't know what to do." She clasped her hands together so tightly that the rings looked like they were cutting off her circulation. "I've wanted to leave Stuart for ages, but I didn't want a long, drawn-out, ugly divorce. And yes, I wanted my fair share of our net worth. Rhett approached me at some event or another a few years ago and was asking about the Cresswell case. I put him off, but a few months later I made him a deal. I told him that if he helped me get a quick and fair divorce settlement from Stuart, that I'd tell him all I knew about Cresswell."

"What exactly did you know about Cresswell?"

She shrugged. "Things. Wives hear stuff sometimes— phone conversations, a few words at dinner, business talk."

"And what things did you hear?" Watching her twist her fingers practically off was driving me crazy, so I tried to keep my gaze on her face instead.

"Stuart found something out, and he didn't go to the authorities. He's the kind of man that would rather hold information in his back pocket and use it when it benefits him the most. But the problem is that he knew that he knew, so he hid it where no one would think to look, then told him it was all okay and that they were buddies and that he wouldn't rat him out."

I was absolutely confused. "Who? Who hid what where?"

She glared at me. "I just told you. Stuart found out what Sonny did and hid the paperwork in his old office in a hole in the drywall in the closet."

"Wait. Sonny Magoo did something illegal during the Cresswell case, and your husband knew about it and hid evidence of it in his office at SMS&C?"

"Yes." She nodded vigorously. "I told Rhett the details and where the files were hidden in the office."

"But how did Sonny Magoo find out that Rhett was onto him?" I mused.

Helen squirmed. "I told him. At the party. I let him know that Rhett was going to expose him, and that he needed to get those files before Rhett did. He went right upstairs to get them, and about fifteen minutes later the police arrived. Sonny didn't come back downstairs for a while, and when he did, he looked really upset and he had pants on that didn't match his tux jacket and his shirt was some cheap cotton thing. I said something to him, and he made me promise to say I was with him the whole time." She clenched her hands together again. "I didn't know Sonny was going to kill him! I just thought he could get to the files first, then Rhett wouldn't have any proof."

"He embezzled money and you tipped him off so he could get away with it?" My voice rose quite a bit at the end of that question.

"Sonny was good guy. It was only five hundred thousand."

I bit my tongue at that. "So how did Rhett manage to help you with your divorce? You said that was your payment for giving him the information on the Cresswell case."

Helen's chin went up. "That's not relevant. He had a few words with Stuart and everything went easy after that. I didn't ask, and he didn't tell."

Wonderful. Maybe there was something in those files that would implicate Stuart Dixon as well. Was the whole darned appellate court crooked? I was beginning to think Rhett Reynolds might be right.

"Did you really have an affair with Rhett Reynolds?" I asked, more out of curiosity than anything else.

She wrinkled her nose. "No. We thought it would be a good way for Stuart to save face. Rhett didn't mind. And I accepted it as the price I paid for an easy divorce."

I stood. "You have to go to the police right now. They've

got something that implicates you in all this. If you go now and tell them what you told me—including that Sonny Magoo asked you to give him an alibi, then things will definitely go easier on you."

Helen remained seated for a few moments, chewing her lip, then she stood. "It's not like I can flee the country or anything. My divorce settlement wasn't *that* big. Plus I just closed on this house and my new car doesn't come in until next week."

For Pete's sake. Could this woman *be* any more shallow? "Do you need a lift to the police station then? Since your car doesn't come in until next week?"

I was being sarcastic, but it went right over Helen's head.

"Oh no. I still have my old car."

She got her keys and her purse, then locked up as I waited on the porch. I'll admit that I called Detective Bettie Page to let her know Helen Dixon knew who murdered Rhett Reynolds and was on her way in. I'll also admit that I followed Helen to the police station and waited half an hour after she walked inside before leaving.

Then I headed home. It was three o'clock on Christmas Eve. I couldn't wait to get home, make some hot chocolate, cuddle with my cat, and knit. Judge Beck would hopefully be home early, and Heather would be bringing Henry and Madison over around after nine o'clock.

But there was one more thing I needed to do.

Irene O'Donnell answered on the first ring. "Tell me you've got some happy Christmas news for me, Carrera."

"I do." I told her the whole story, finishing just as I turned down my street.

"That's the best present I've had in years," Irene said. "Just fax me the final invoice whenever you all get back in the office after the holidays and charge it on the card I gave you."

She didn't even ask how much it was. It reminded me a

bit of Helen Dixon and her comment that an embezzlement of five hundred thousand dollars wasn't a big deal. I was so glad this case was over. I was so glad to be back home with my cat and my house, and the people I cared about.

"Merry Christmas, Irene," I told her, hoping she didn't fall over in shock when she got the invoice.

Inside, Taco ran to greet me, informing me that he hadn't eaten in weeks and was wasting away. I let him outside, then headed into the kitchen to pour his kibble. In the corner was Rhett Reynolds' ghost.

"It's done," I told him. "Ruby found the USB drive, and the police have it now. Plus Helen Dixon is going to testify. I'm pretty sure Sonny Magoo is going to be spending Christmas behind bars, especially because I don't think he'll be able to be arraigned and post bail before Monday."

The shadowy figure in the corner of my kitchen seemed to nod. Then he faded away. Gone. I was a little bummed because of all the ghosts who'd been pestering me this year, he was the most polite.

I turned to put the cat food back in the cabinet and some writing on the frost-covered window caught my eye. It was Ruby's name with a heart drawn around it.

"She knows," I whispered, even though the ghost had long gone. "She knows you love her. And she'll never forget it."

CHAPTER 17

I'd heard stories of kids waking their parents up at some uncivilized hour of the morning to go open Christmas presents, but that clearly didn't apply to teenagers. Judge Beck was downstairs before me, but the house was far too silent for Madison and Henry to have arisen yet. The smell of coffee greeted me as I walked down the stairs. I heard the clink of a mug, the soft whisper of slippered feet. As I came around the corner I saw Judge Beck wearing a pair of pajamas with some anime character on them, his hair tousled. He held two coffee mugs in his hand and turned to greet me with a smile.

"I heard you coming down the stairs."

I took one of the coffee mugs from him and added a splash of cream. "This is the definition of getting old, you know. We're awake before the kids."

"Did you want some prune juice in that? Maybe a Geritol?"

"No thanks. Let's go sit by the tree and talk about our aches and pains as we drink our coffee. Maybe we can complain about people on our lawn, or discuss the last time we had a bowel movement."

The judge choked on his coffee, sputtering and spewing coffee across the island. I waited until he finally got control of his breathing, then continued.

"My sciatica's been acting up a bit lately. How about you?"

"Think I might need new reading glasses. I've been having to hold things at arm's length again to see them." He bit back a smile, trying desperately to appear serious. "I pooped first thing this morning, by the way."

This time it was me choking on my coffee. This was what Madison would have called TMI, but it was hysterical.

"Heavens! Such language!" I fanned my face. "I'll have you know that I tend to take my daily constitutionals directly after my morning coffee."

"I'm glad to hear you're regular." He nodded. "It's important at our age to move our bowels on a schedule."

I heard a strangled gasp behind me and turned to see Madison in blue fuzzy pajamas, her hair in a messy topknot.

"Seriously? I come down for a magical Christmas morning and you both are discussing pooping?"

The judge waved a stern finger at his daughter. "Constitutional. Or bowel movements. Our Kay takes exception to the vulgarity of the word 'poop.'"

I really didn't, but it was worth it to see Madison's outraged expression.

"It's poop, Dad. And I don't want to hear about it."

"So when do *you* move your bowels, Mads?" Judge Beck asked, a devilish twinkle in his hazel eyes. "Or do teenage girls not poop? Maybe your excrement is all rainbows and glitter and smells like roses."

"Dad!" she shrieked, covering her ears. Then she laughed and launched herself into his arms, nearly spilling his coffee. "Merry Christmas, Dad."

He gripped her tight, his head bent over hers. "Merry Christmas, my Maddy-Mads."

I heard the edge of tears in his voice and it made my own vision a bit misty. They separated, and I was surprised to find myself a recipient of a similar hug from Madison.

She pulled away, and the look she gave me made me choke back tears.

"Go wake your brother so we can open presents," Judge Beck told her with a smile. "Then we'll have that French toast casserole you made."

She rolled her eyes. "I'll get the little monster up and moving. Don't open anything without us!"

She ran up the stairs and we took our coffee into the parlor. I started some holiday music, flicked the lights on for the tree, then took a seat beside the judge on the sofa. We sipped our coffee in silence, watching the blinking tree lights reflect off the ornaments. The sounds of thumping footsteps overhead and yelling teenagers harmonized with the orchestral sounds of "Silent Night" in a strange fashion. I felt warm. Content. Happy.

In short order the kids were downstairs and we were tearing through wrapping paper. Madison was thrilled with her scarf, and actually hugged Henry over the coral leather wristlet he'd given her. Judge Beck was wearing his leather jacket over his threadbare Hard Rock Cafe t-shirt, and exclaiming over the new putter from Henry.

I opened a box so heavy that I needed to get down on the floor to tear the paper off it. The box showed a picture of a small cold frame, a dozen thriving tomato plants inside.

"Do you like it?" Henry shyly asked. "I heard you say you wish you had one. I thought you could get an early start on herbs next year and grow those tomato varieties you wanted from seed. Dad said he'd help me put it together."

"I love it," I told Henry, pulling him in for a hug. "And I

expect you to help me go through seed catalogues this winter, picking out what we should grow."

He beamed. "Totally."

"Mine. Open mine next." Madison shoved a box into my hands, nearly dancing with excitement. I opened it and saw the cat-hat, a pair of buttery soft, black leather driving gloves, and a membership notification for a wine club.

"Mom helped me buy the wine thing because I'm too young," she said. "I thought it would be cool for your Friday porch parties, or maybe when you and Dad are working late one night."

I smiled, my heart feeling as if it would burst. "Thank you, Madison. I love the gloves, and you know how much I love wine. This is such a thoughtful gift."

Henry seemed genuinely thrilled over the book I'd given him, immediately sitting over to the side and paging through it, commenting on various furniture styles in Colonial times. Judge Beck opened my gift and I held my breath, suddenly nervous.

He pulled out the antique watch, the one that no longer worked, the one that had been set at eleven o'clock since my grandfather had died. He turned it over to see the engraving and read, "Time is the most precious gift we have." Then he took out the picture frame. Turning it on, he watched as it cycled through pictures of Madison and Henry throughout the year. There were pictures of them building their raft, in the hot tub, at their sporting events, cuddling Taco. There were pictures of the four of us at Halloween, at Thanksgiving, and decorating the Christmas tree.

A whole host of unreadable expressions flickered across the judge's face. Did he understand what was behind this gift? It wasn't just the symbolism of the antique watch, it was the pictures of his children—and of the four of us.

It was far too soon for any sort of declaration on my part,

and honestly I was too scared and uncertain to even know where my feelings lay as far as the judge was concerned, but I wanted him to know there was a place in my heart for him, and in my world, that included my home.

"Kay...this is wonderful. Thank you." He leaned over and hugged me and for a second I froze. Then I melted into him, feeling the warmth of him around me, breathing in the scent of soap and sandalwood and the distinctive scent of a man's skin.

Henry opened up a small box and let out a whoop, waving three plane tickets in the air. "We're going! We're going!"

"Skiing?" Madison snatched the tickets from her brother and looked at them. "Dad, this is awesome!"

"I already cleared it with your mother," he told them. "And the school will be putting together packets for the week you're missing. I'll expect both of you to be doing homework every evening. No exceptions."

They both ignored him. Madison grabbed her phone and pulled up the website for the resort, then she and Henry started commenting on all the things they wanted to do on their winter vacation.

I got up and went to the front door, Taco at my heels. Opening it up, I shouted in mock dismay.

"Darn it! Taco snuck out the door. Madison, can you help me get him back in?"

Madison was one of the few people Taco would come to when he'd made an escape to the great outdoors. I wasn't sure if she'd protest or not, given that it was Christmas morning and she was in charge of warming up the French toast casserole she'd made last night, but she cheerfully said she'd be right there and dashed into the kitchen.

I shivered as I walked out onto the front porch, Judge Beck following close behind me. In a few seconds, Madison appeared with a bag of treats in her hand. She shook it, calling for Taco as she looked around.

"Who's here?" she frowned, looking at the car in our driveway. It was a bright red Acura sedan, about ten years old, but clean and shiny, and carefully inspected by the employees at Turn Of The Wrench auto repair.

"No one." Judge Beck watched his daughter, grinning when the look of confusion on her face was replaced by one of eagerness.

"Who...whose car is that?" Her voice squeaked as she pointed.

The judge pulled a set of keys out of his pajama pants pocket and handed them to her. "I believe it's your car."

Madison screamed. I swear I think dogs in a two-mile radius heard her. Then she screamed again, hugged her father, and raced down the steps through the snow in her pajamas and slippers.

"It's from both me *and* your mother," Judge Beck called after her. "Make sure you thank her when she picks you up this afternoon."

My eyebrows went up and I looked at him. "So you changed your mind?"

"I decided that my being petty doesn't help anyone. It definitely doesn't help Madison. No matter what happens in mine and Heather's lives, we'll always need to cooperate and work together for the benefit of our children. There will be times we don't agree, and times when old wounds are going to open and ache again, but in the end I want both Henry and Madison to know they're loved by both of us. I don't want them thinking they need to play monkey-in-the-middle to appease parents who are constantly trying to one-up each other. I don't want them worrying about how we'll act when we have to be together during a wedding or grandchild's birthday party. There are enough things for my kids to worry about in life. Their parents' fractured marriage shouldn't be one of them."

I agreed. The rest of the day we spent eating French toast casserole, eating cookies, eating candy, and sprawling on the basement couch in a sugar coma to watch movies. Madison and I had collaborated on the dinner so around four o'clock we sat down to eat traditional ham and mashed potatoes, cheese fritters, honey-sweetened carrot puree, and a five-bean salad. The judge and Henry handled the dishes, while I knitted and Madison went upstairs to get a few things together to take to her mom's.

There was always a feeling of let-down once the sun set on Christmas. All the build-up, all the anticipation, but the event always seemed to be over so fast. I put the holiday music back on to help me ease the transition back to normal life, picked up the remaining scraps of wrapping paper to throw out, and went into the kitchen.

Taco had finished his dinner and was licking a paw. The dishes were cleaned and put away. Judge Beck was out front talking to Heather and saying goodbye to Madison and Henry. They'd be back Sunday evening, but I always missed them so when they were gone. And next year would be especially difficult since it would be Heather's turn to have them for the holiday.

Determined not to let such a wonderful day end on a sad note, I put a cup of cider in the microwave, adding a few spices once it was hot. The moonlight reflecting off the snow lit up my back yard. On impulse, I grabbed a blanket from the living room and headed out the back door, hot cider in my hand and Taco at my heels.

The blanket didn't quite keep the cold from the metal chair from seeping through to my legs, but at least my hands were warm from the steaming mug. I watched Taco hop off into the snow, shaking his paws and yowling in annoyance at the wet white clinging to his fur. After a few feet he was back, jumping into my lap to curl up in the blanket.

I sipped my cider, mesmerized by the cold serenity of the night. Even the faint sound of the back door and Judge Beck sliding onto the chair next to me disrupted the peaceful quiet.

An envelope appeared at my elbow. I took it and looked questioningly up at the judge.

"I didn't want to give this to you while the kids were here," he said softly, as if he was reluctant to disturb the silence of the night. "They're refundable, so if you say 'no' it's not a problem. I just thought…I wanted… But if you can't get out of work, or if you think it would be too awkward, or it's not your thing, it's okay."

He looked rather flustered, and I had no idea what the heck he was babbling about, so I opened the envelope, assuming there would be some enlightenment within.

It was a plane ticket and a brochure for a ski resort—the same ski resort he and Madison and Henry were going to. The same week they were going.

I stared at the brochure, suddenly mute.

"The kids would love it if you came with us," he said. "I…I would love it if you came with us. We'll have a lot of fun. I booked a suite in the lodge with a fireplace and a balcony overlooking the slopes. Henry and I can share a room, and you and Madison can share the other. There's two queen beds in each room, and private bathrooms for each, but I can get you a separate room if you think that would be better."

I didn't think it would be better, but all the words I wanted to say didn't seem to want to come out.

"But…" The judge clenched his hands together. "You're family, Kay. We think of you as family. *I* think of you as family. I want you to come with us. I want you to stay in the suite with us. If you're comfortable with that, I mean."

I reached out and put my hand over his clenched ones, finally finding my voice. "Thank you. I want to go, and I definitely want to stay with you—I mean with all of you. To room with Madison, I mean. Thank you for including me. This is the best Christmas present I've had in a very long time."

He smiled, unclenching his hands to entwine his fingers with mine. "So there's one more thing I need to ask you."

I was family. He considered me family. He'd invited me to go on a vacation with him and his children. Suddenly the moon and stars seemed brighter, Taco on my lap seemed warmer and softer. The judge's hand in mine felt so very right, as if it belonged there.

"Yes?" I asked, somewhat breathlessly.

His smile widened into a grin. "Are you a ski person, or a snowboard person? Because according to Henry, only old fogies like us ski."

* * *

THERE'S MORE Kay and friends coming your way with Book 10 in the Locust Point Mystery Series. To be notified of new releases, subscribe at https:// libbyhowardbooks.com/subscribe/

ALSO BY LIBBY HOWARD

Locust Point Mystery Series:

The Tell All

Junkyard Man

Antique Secrets

Hometown Hero

A Literary Scandal

Root of All Evil

A Grave Situation

Last Supper

A Midnight Clear

Fire and Ice

ACKNOWLEDGMENTS

Special thanks to Lyndsey Lewellen for cover design and typography, and to Jennifer Cosham for copyediting.

ABOUT THE AUTHOR

Libby Howard lives in a little house in the woods with her sons and two exuberant bloodhounds. She occasionally knits, occasionally bakes, and occasionally manages to do a load of laundry. Most of her writing is done in a bar where she can combine work with people-watching, a decent micro-brew, and a plate of Old Bay wings.

For more information:
libbyhowardbooks.com/